MAMA DON'T LIKE UGLY

By

Rekaya Gibson

ISBN-13: 978-0-9887382-1-8
ISBN-10: 098873821X

Mama Don't Like Ugly is a work of fiction. Names, characters, places, and incidents are either products of the author's imagination or are used fictitiously. Any resemblance to actual persons, living or dead, business establishments, events or locales is entirely coincidental.

Published by
Gibson Girl Publishing Company, LLC
P. O. Box 11203
Newport News, VA 23601
www.gibsongirlpublishingcompany.com

Edited by Leila Jefferson
Interior Designed by Gibson Girl Publishing Company, LLC
Cover Designed by Gibson Girl Publishing Company, LLC

Library of Congress Control Number: 2012955637

Printed in the United States of America

Dedication

Shirley Mae Joshua
(1942 – 2010)

Acknowledgements

I would like to thank my family, friends, and fans for this amazing journey. I could not have done it without your support. You are awesome!

MAMA DON'T

LIKE UGLY

Chapter 1

"Please, help me! Help me!"

"Miss Calhoun, please stop moving," the doctor calmly pleaded.

"I cannot help it. You got to get this baby out."

"Oh, Lord…Oh….Jesus, help me."

"Stop pushing!"

"I'll take that epidural now, I'll take it. Please!"

"It's too late. You should have taken it when we offered it to you. Grab her hands!"

The nurse and the nurse's assistant each took an arm. They wrestled with her at first before getting a strong hold. Once she learned that she could not fight them off, she settled down a little.

"Please, stop it! Miss Calhoun!"

Hey…Whoa… I'm moving around way too much. What is going on out there? What is all the noise about? And, who in the hell left the gate open? Is anyone listening to me? .

"I see the top of his head!" the doctor exclaimed.

He? Who is he? I did not know who he was or who he was referring to out there. All I knew was the liquid that once surrounded me was now subsided and I was upside down.

"Come on, little guy. You can do it."

"1, 2, 3…push!" the nurse told Mama.

"I am, dammit!"

"1, 2, 3…push!"

That sounds like a fun game. 1, 2, 3…push! I'll say it with them next time.

"1, 2, 3…pushhhhh!"

"Yahhhhhhhhhhhhhhhhhhhhhh!"

What the…that sound hurt my ears and I am moving awfully fast.

"Here he comes. One more big push and it should do. Ready?"

No, I am not ready. Why are you tugging on me?

"1, 2, 3…pushhhh!"

"Got it."

What does he mean got it? He did not just catch a football, and what is he going to do with those gigantic scissors.

"He is not crying," the doctor whispered.

Slap!

That hurt, goddammit! How would you like it if I slapped your ass!

"He didn't even cry. He is already a tough guy."

He clipped the cord dangling from my stomach. "Wan! Wan! Wan!"

"Doctor, it's a girl," the nurse commented.

"What?"

"Girl." The nurse pointed between my legs.

"You don't say? Miss Calhoun, you have a little girl."

"What?" she replied in a groggy voice.

"It's a female. We made a mistake. You have another little girl."

"Great, just great." Mama did not have an ounce of enthusiasm in her voice.

"See?" The doctor held me high in the air. Too bad I did not get a nosebleed, I would have made it a point to spray all over him.

My mama did not even open her eyes to look, she seemed too exhausted.

"We will take her now, doctor."

As soon as he passed me to the nurse, I stop wailing. She placed me on a soft towel and sponged my belly, arms and legs. She pushed a suction thing into my nose and I tried moving her hand, but I could not reach it. Plus, she shifted a lot quicker than me. I did not cry because I was tough as nails. A different nurse put a multi-color hat on my head. *Thank goodness, I am getting cold.* Then, I felt someone playing with my toes. I moved my feet around to see if she would stop. She did not. Finally, something soft touched them. It caressed my ankles, too. *Let me look.* I attempted to move my head, but I could not see anything. Did my milk belly blocked the way or I was just stiff? Whatever it was, my feet cherish the warmth. *Oh look, a blanket. I wonder what I need with it. Nurse…nurse…* I tried reading her name badge, but I could not focus my eyes, a glassy film covered them. In addition, I could not read. Oh well, she was doing a great job. She wrapped me in a thermal blanket like a burrito – nice and snug.

"Are you ready to see your mother?" she asked me.

Yes.

"Here you go, Miss Calhoun, your baby girl."

Hi, Mama! You are so beautiful. I cannot wait to touch your silky, black hair and trace your thick eyebrows with my fingers. Then, I will give you lots of kisses on your smooth cheeks. She had pronounced African- and Asian- American features. Though she had a rough delivery, she still looked vibrant and youthful.

"Coo. Coo."

Mama opened her eyes and glanced at me. She stared for a moment, as if she was trying to figure out whom I was. Then, she turned her head.

"Miss Calhoun, it's your baby. Are you still asleep?"

The woman put me on her bosom. Mama turned onto her right side. I roll toward the nurse and she caught me just in time.

Mama, it is me.

"Madame, don't you want to hold your baby?"

"No, get her out of here!"

"But, Miss Calhoun…"

"Now!"

"Waaaa!" It was the second time that I cried and it felt as though it would not be my last. It was then that I knew my life would be a living hell.

"It's alright, precious." The redhead lady rocked me gently. "I'll give you some dinner so your mother has time to rest."

ƐƐƐ

The hospital released Mama and me the next day. Good thing my Aunt Mildred, Mama's sister, came to get me, otherwise, I would still be in the incubator kicking it with the other "homies." Mama was still exhausted and depressed. The hospital staff kept saying that she had postpartum depression and she would get over it soon. Aunt Mildred called it neglect and ridiculed mama for having me. Mama refused because she did not believe in abortion. She considered putting me up for adoption, but Aunt Mildred talked her out of it. She laid a guilt trip on Mama about taking care of her responsibility and using the whole, "What would our mama say about this," discussion.

"Miss Calhoun, you have one more thing to do before leaving the hospital. You need to fill out the baby's birth certificate," the nurse told her and handed her a pen.

Mama gripped it and scribbled something on paper. I waited on her to say something, but she never did. I had no clue what my mama sounded like in person. I heard echoes in the womb, but I could not make out sentences.

Aunt Mildred picked up the form and read some of it. "Birth of Dana Rae Calhoun, birthplace Nautica, Louisiana, father's name, unknown." Aunt Mildred rolled her eyes and handed the document to the midwife. "I'll carry the baby."

One nurse held the door, while the other pushed mama in a wheelchair. As soon as the group reached the exit doors, a little girl came running toward my aunt. Mama's live-in boyfriend, Carl, sat in the driver seat as if he was a zombie. He did not say anything and mama did not speak to him. They met at "The White Horse Lounge" when she was eight months pregnant. She was there celebrating her friend's birthday. He asked her to dance and the rest was history. After one month, he moved in the house.

"She is so cute," the nurse's aid chimed. "I wish my daughter had hair like hers. She has good hair."

"Let me see! Let me see the baby!" She jumped up and down.

Aunt Mildred held me down by her waist and kneeled over.

"You see your sister, Kelly?" she asked her.

"Yes." She gave me a kiss on the forehead.

Hi, sister! She is bigger and prettier version of the kids that I shared a room with last night.

"That's the only person you see, Kelly? What about your mama?" Mama mentioned.

Wow, she speaks.

"Hi, Mama," Kelly sang.

Mama reached out to hug her daughter. "You've been a good girl?"

"Yes."

Kelly climbed into the back of the car and around the car seat. The nurse, certified in car seat installation, showed Aunt Mildred how to buckle me in safely and properly. It was required by law to have a safety seat for an infant before leaving the hospital. I listened to the conversation with my eyes closed. I heard Mama sighing in the front seat; she was obviously ready to go. I guess she did not have the gall to say anything crazy to Aunt Mildred or she would have put her in her place. All the sounds got on my nerves, so I decided to take a nap.

ϵϵϵ

"Baby. Baby."

I heard a soft voice. I opened my eyes and looked in the direction of the sound. It was hard for me to move my head, but I managed to adjust it slightly to the right. My sister was peeking over the bassinet. She pats my belly three times and smiled. I gave her an intense look.

"What are you doing in here?" Mama asked Kelly.

It is Mama. Hi, Mama!

"I'm talking to Dana."

Mama picked Kelly up so that she could get a better view. I laughed at both of them, they looked like funhouse characters.

"Kelly, take a good look at your sister. You looking?" She nodded. "You will always look prettier than her."

"I'm pretty, Mama?"

9

"Yes, you are. Don't let anyone tell you different. Do you hear me?" She moved her head. "I cannot hear your head, Kelly."

"Yes."

Mama put her down. "Now, stop bothering your sister, Kelly, and go play."

"Awe," she remarked and skipped out the room.

I think Mama is going to pick me up. My turn is next.

Mama looked down on me with gloomy eyes. As she leaned in closer, I got more excited. *Hurray! Mama is going to hold me.* She put her left hand around the top of the bed and the right at the bottom.

"Did you see how gorgeous your sister Kelly looks? Well, you will never look as pretty. Your skin will get darker and crusty as you get older. You will look like a spook, society will confirm that for you. That is why Kelly will always be my favorite child. Her skin is olive, like mine. I know it was stupid of me to get pregnant by Ray Townsend in the first place, but I heard some great things about him in the bedroom. Yes, my mama warned me about those darkies, but I did not listen. You will never know him because I did not tell him about you. You will soar to nothing and Kelly will amount to something. Perhaps, I will give you to Mildred since she said you look like her and she loves you so much. No one will ever believe that you are my child, anyway."

"Tracey!" Mildred called.

"I am in here."

"There you are. Did you hold your baby yet?"

Mama blinked her eyes at her sister, then she glanced back at me. "I'm not ready."

"You need to get ready. I cannot do this forever," Aunt Mildred told her with a stern voice. "Ain't that right, Dana?" Aunt Mildred tickled my stomach.

Mama grinned, then went into the other room. Aunt Mildred checked my diaper, picked me up with safe hands, and gave me dinner.

She always brings treats when I see her, unlike that mama lady. She sure does ramble a lot and fast. I could not make out what she was saying to me earlier because I kept drifting in-and-out of sleep. Something about pretty, favorite child, and loves you. Oh well…it must not have been important or I would have stayed awake. Umm, umm, this is good milk.

€€€

"I have to run out to get some diapers and formula. Can you watch your daughter for at least a hour?" Aunt Mildred asked mama, however, she did not respond. Then, she decided to say something to Carl who grossed her out with his burly belly. "Carl, did you hear me?"

"Yes, I heard you, and so did Tracey. That is not my child."

"I know, Carl. I know. You let us know that every day. I am telling anyone in the room who wants to listen. I figure you can be Tracey's backup. Is that alright?"

He moaned, so she took it as a yes. I lie in my bed listening to the conversation, the television, and Kelly singing over in the corner. I catnapped when the house was quiet, which was usually at night.

Carl let out a burp. "I need more beer. I am running to the store, too. I will be right back," Carl told Kelly since she was the only one who responded to him on the regular.

"Okay." She continued singing. "The mouse ran up…"

I could not take it any longer, so I tuned her out. I start humming my own tune, just random noises. Kelly's singing got louder the closer that she moved toward me. Perhaps, she would play with me.

Ouch! Ouch! Stop it! Stop it! Kelly, why are you pinching me on my upper left arm? I let out a piercing cry, hoping Mama would stop her from hurting me. *Please, Mama. Please, do something about Kelly.* I tried rolling over, but it did not work. I moved my arm fast, but not fast enough.

"Mama, I don't want to pinch Dana anymore!" Kelly retorted. Then, the pricks stop.

"Do it one more time, Kelly. Do it one more time for mama."

"But, Mama, I don't…"

"Kelly, I will get you that shinny red tricycle that we saw yesterday."

Kelly hesitated for a moment. "One more, that's it."

"Okay, make sure it is long and hard as you can. Make me proud, baby."

With my liquid filled eyes, I stared Kelly down in disbelief. That pretty girl that I knew as my sister caused me pain. The worst part was that Mama put her up to it and cheered her on like a fan at a sporting event. Kelly reached for my arm one last time and pretended to do it again. She put her little hands on my shoulder and pat me. I calm down a little; however, it took several minutes to regain my normal breathing pattern. By then, I guess the tyrant got tired of torturing her baby girl. She sat on the couch laughing at something on television that did not seem funny. The fakeness annoyed me and sent chills up my spine.

"I'm back!" Aunt Mildred yelled over the blaring tube. She walked over to the bassinet to check on me. She looked down with a loving smile, and I felt relieved to see a friendly, soothing face. She sensed something odd and touched my soaked clothing. It tipped her off that I had been crying. "Why is the baby wet? She's been crying?"

"Yes, a little, but I took care of her. She just needed a little tender loving care," Mama responded with glee. Aunt Mildred looked at her with suspicion. As she walked toward the kitchen to put the groceries away, she studied Mama's body language. When she returned, she gave her the same look. She picked me up and kissed my cheeks. I was barely awake.

"Let's get you cleaned up, my baby," she murmured. I open my eyes a little to see who picked me up. When I noticed it was my aunt, I closed them.

€€€

"What are you doing, Mildred?" My mama asked.

My eyes fluttered at the sound of her voice.

"Shhh…you are going to wake the baby. I was reading your daughter a bedtime story."

"But, she is sleeping."

"So."

"Why don't you come in the living room with the rest of us? We are watching a good movie."

"Let me tell you something, sister." Mildred stopped rocking the chair. I wiggled a little so that I could adjust my position. Then, I notice more movement. I opened my right eye for a second. The next thing I knew, I was in my bed. The cushions hugged my small body. I was ready to call it a day. "The next time I leave Dana in your care and return and she has marks on her arm, I am taking her out of this house."

Mama pretended to be startled with her comments. "What are you talking about?"

"You know exactly what I am talking about. The baby's arm was red when I got here, now it's blue."

"Let me see."

Mildred stood in front of the doorway to block mama from approaching the bed. "Don't you dare touch her!"

Mama slid to the right. "It's my baby, I can see…" Mildred shoved mama backwards. "You better back off Tracey." They eyeballed each other for a minute.

I sucked my lips, searching for milk. I heard too much noise, but I was too tired to open my heavy eyes again.

They both look in my direction. "Leave this room, Tracey, while you still can." Mama poked out her lips and shook her head up and down. She walked away, then turned around to say something, but decided against it. She moseyed on down the hall.

"Now, where were we?" Aunt Mildred opened the children's book to page five and hovered over me to complete the story. "Oh, *yes*, there *are* French fries in heaven!" she read with glee. I beamed in my sleep as I transcended to my own French fry heaven.

€€€

Six weeks had past and Mama still had not touched me. She was back to talking, gossiping and cussing folks out. Aunt Mildred took care of me – day and night - like a mother. I was not a fussy baby, I just whined a little when I needed food, my diaper changed, and a little attention. Kelly played with me when she had the time. She was too busy with games, coloring, and attending parties with the other three year olds. I took frequent naps out of sheer boredom.

There was a crash.

"Mill, you okay? Mill? Mill! Oh, Lord. Call 9-1-1, Mill collapsed," Mama yelled to Carl, who entered the room to get a view. He ran back into the living room to retrieve the phone. Carl's voice carried much anger with the person on the receiving end. He kept saying he did not know. I wondered why?

I was in the bassinet in the kitchen. I tried sitting up to find out what was going on to no avail. I stared at the white ceiling and listened.

"Mill, oh, Mill, wake up! Please, wake up!"

"Come on, Tracey, get up. Get off the floor," Carl told her.

"Shut up! Shut up! She is my sister and I can do what I want. Shut the hell up. Did you call the paramedics? Where are they?"

"I did. They are on the way."

I heard sirens in the far distance. I could hear the piercing sound increasing as it got closer. Soon, folks would be gathering outside to figure out what was going on inside our home. Someone would make up a crazy story and start telling the neighborhood, until the real news came out.

The front screen door hit the frame. It was Kelly and the next-door neighbor, Bonnie, holding hands. They walked into the kitchen.

"I heard…" the neighbor began.

"Auntie M!" Kelly cried.

"Get my baby out of here. Get her out of here, now!" Mama yelled.

She picked up Kelly and shielded her face by pressing her head into her shoulder. She headed back to her house. No one paid attention to me. I lie there, crying in silent. Tears rolled down each cheek simultaneously. They would stop at the edge of my ears, waiting on another wave. The left drop would fall first, then the right. They landed inside my ears, clogging them up. The irritation did not bother me, however, the coldness in the air did. *What's going to happen to me now?*

Chapter 2

Mama finally assumed her role as a mother and since I had a routine, it made it easier for her - for the most part. She started holding and feeding me, however, she lacked regular diaper changes. I cried to get her attention, but she did not respond.

"Yuck, Dana, you stink." Kelly walked past to let me know, and then she went to tell mama and Carl. They did not say or do anything. Mama continued cooking and Carl turned up the television louder. I was going on eight hours without a fresh bottom. My bedding, clothes, and diaper were soiled and wet. Every time I moved, the poop and pee slid out. After awhile, I stopped blubbering because I got tired of hearing myself. No one else was around to pick up the slack.

Carl was not much of a babysitter or taking care of his own children. He had seven by three baby mamas that he did not see. He chose not to work because he did not want to pay child support. He played video games all day or went around the corner to 'kick it with his boys' as he put it. What my mama saw in him, I would never know. She was an educated, professional woman; she could totally do better.

Mama came into the room waving a bottle. "Here you go, Dana. Awe man, look at you." Mama frowned and I laughed at her funny face. "You have shit all over the place, including your fingers. Goddammit, I better get you cleaned up."

Mama lifted me up away from her body and rushed me into the bathroom, almost knocking Carl down. "Do me a favor. Remove everything off that bed, put it in the laundry, and wash down the mattress with bleach. Look in the closet for a new blanket and sheets, and put them on before I get her out the tub." Carl huffed and went toward the garage to retrieve the chlorine.

When mama took me into the bedroom, I started falling asleep. Carl pushed the bassinet into the room and placed it next to the window. "You might want to wait awhile before putting her in because the bleach smell is strong," he told Mama.

"She'll be fine."

He shrugged his shoulders and left. Mama put my Pamper on, sprinkled powder on my chest, and put me in a nightgown. I felt fresh. I gobbled my milk and went to sleepy town. As soon as Mama laid me down, I inhaled the intense odor. It tickled my nose, so I touched it, thinking I could remove the annoyance. It kept playing with me to the point where I could not sleep. Then, I start coughing. My throat burned and the sensation traveled to my nose and eyes. I felt as though I was suffocating. I cried.

"What's wrong now, Dana? I just bathed you and fed you," Mama commented as she glanced down at me. I wiggled. I cried. She still did nothing.

"I told you that aroma was potent. Can't you tell? She is probably bothered by it. Just put her in our bed for now," Carl advised. Mama did not like Carl's authoritative response.

"She will be alright." Mama shoved the bed closer to the window. "The draft from the window should help. There." She marched out.

"Unbelievable," Carl retorted. He sat in the chair next to me and tried to sooth my nerves by shifting the bed around gently. I tried fighting the fumes, but they beat me. The breeze did not help matters, it gave me a chill. I sneezed. "Bless you, baby," Carl replied. I guess he could not bear to see me in distress, so he removed me. He stroked my back for a while and laid me on their bed. Mama walked in and glared at him.

"Tomorrow is a busy day, I hope you get a good night sleep," she reminded him.

I slept for three hours. When I opened my eyes, Mama was focused on me. She turned over and I began to cry. I sounded faint even though it was the scream for help. Something was asphyxiating me. It was covering my entire body and it was heavy on my nose. It reminded me of a blanket, but it had a perfume smell to it.

"Tracey! Tracey! Move back! Move it! You are on the baby. Move your ass!" Carl yelled and heaved her.

"What?" she asked in confusion while moving.

"You were on Dana."

"Oh. Okay." She pretended to hear him. Carl pushed the middle of her back in anger. She mumbled several broken words, similar to a sleepy person. He had no clue what she said. He returned me to my bed.

"I don't want anything to happen to the kumquat." I was too tired to put up a fuss about the stench or almost dying. Carl stood over me as I drifted off to sleep within seconds. He was my new protector. He kept a sharp eye on me in the days leading up to Aunt Mildred's funeral. Every day since the ambulance took her away, I wished that she would return. I missed her so much and hoped to see her again someday.

ЄЄЄ

Everyone was dressed up nicely. I had on my yellow lace dress with matching bloomers and white bobby socks with black, patent leather shoes. I had a yellow and white baby barrette in my hair. Kelly had a similar outfit, but hers was a different color. Carl had a gray suit with a purple tie and handkerchief. He was handsome for a big guy. He wore a neat goatee with a bald head, standing six foot three with his weight mainly in his gut. Mama's beauty radiated in her black and white sleeveless dress. We resembled a good-looking family in spite of its dysfunction.

When we arrived at the church, parishioners greeted us with hugs and kisses. "Ya'll look so nice. Oh, Kelly, you are so pretty in pink, and I love your hair," Sister Agnes mentioned in a cheerful voice, touching Kelly's long ponytail.

"Thank you, sister," Mama responded and kept

24

walking into the church. The escort took us to our seats. Mama handed me to Carl so that she could take care of last minute details with Pastor Cherry. I did what I do best, take naps.

"Yes! Amen! Glory to God! Hallelujah! Thank You, Lord!" I woke to the sound of multiple voices. The musicians begin to play and the choir sang. I felt the drums thumping in my heart and sopranos ringing in my ears. After two minutes, I heard mama singing off key. *Can't she hear herself?* She stood and then rocked me to the beat. *I cannot wait until this song is over; this moving side-to-side is making me queasy.* She sat down when I start burping. She swayed forward and backward on the pew until the final beat. However, the crowd continued praising God. The pastor encouraged them with his words until his deacons were ready to pass the collection plates. Mama did not put anything in because she left her checkbook at home. Carl passed the buck much quicker than she did. She was anxious to move on with the program and to see her sister one final time. Pastor Cherry noticed the frustration on her face, so he quickened the pace.

The procession to view the body started with Mama. She held me close to her bosom, protecting me from the sights. Then, she turned me around to see my Aunt Mildred lying in her casket. I knew it was her, but I could not figure out why she did not move. She did not hug me nor kiss me like she always did.

"See, Dana, there is your Aunt Mildred." Her skin looked different. The make-up was three shades lighter than her skin, making her look like a ghost with bright red lips. She was dressed in a black, button-down dress with a white lace collar. Her hair looked like a bird's nest that had fallen from a tree and landed in a ditch.

"Give your aunt a kiss." Mama put me near her face so that I could kiss her. When I did not reach, she moved my head down further.

I began crying. *I do not want to kiss her, get me out of here.* I slobbered on her cheek. I did not mean to do it. I cried more.

"Oh, Mill, I miss you. Oh, Lord, why? Why, Lord?" Mama cried.

"Someone, get the baby," I heard a male voice chime. Carl ran up and grabbed me out of Mama's arms. He took me outside so that I would not disturb the others. Plus, he did not want to be there himself. I felt better, even though the image of Aunt Mildred was still in my head. I cooed at him because he had stepped up his responsibility in caring for me.

The limousines pulled up to take us to the graveyard. Carl entered the building to see how much longer the service would take. Folks passed us by, but no one said anything to him or anything about me. He saw Mama surrounded by people, her eyes puffy from crying. Carl sympathized with her.

"Sister Agnes, can you hold Dana for a moment? I need to let Tracey know that the limo is ready." He handed me over before getting a response.

"Well…um...I guess."

"Thank you."

"My, isn't that dress just darling on you," she told me.

This woman disturbs me, but I do not know why.

"Sister Agnes, whose baby are you holding?" someone asked.

"Tracey Calhoun's."

"Really?"

"I know, right?"

The woman walked off laughing. "Did you see that baby?" I heard her say.

Who are these people? Where is Carl? I even wondered where my Mama was, which was rare. I did not like unfamiliar people.

I started crying again. I figured crying might get me away from the church lady.

"Dana, what's wrong?" Kelly inquired. *Too bad I cannot talk, otherwise, I will explain to her how Sister Agnes smells like fish tacos and how her body language lets me know that she does not want to be bothered.*

Mama walked past Sister Agnes without even acknowledging me. "Ms. Calhoun, here is your baby. Miss Calhoun?" She got into the car and shut the door.

"I'll take her, Madame. Tracey is not feeling so well today," Carl told her.

"I understand, I'll see you in a minute. Do you want me to take Kelly with me?"

"That's okay. She can ride with us." He kissed Sister Agnes on the forehead. She grinned and promised to bring her famous lemon pound cake to the house.

"Bye!" Kelly sang and waved to her.

ϵϵϵ

"Our Father, who art in heaven, hallowed be thy name. Thy kingdom come. Thy will be done, on earth, as it is in heaven. Give us this day, our daily bread, and forgive us our trespasses, as we forgive those who trespass against us, and lead us not into temptation, but deliver us from evil. For thine is the kingdom, and the power, and the glory, forever and ever. Amen." Pastor Cherry recited the Lord's Prayer.

The casket lowered into the ground. Mama wept for her favorite sister. Carl tried to clutch her as he held me. He wore the pants in the relationship that day. Kelly grasped Mama's hand tight.

"Mildred! Mildred!" Mama pulled away from Carl and he almost dropped me. I was unscathed. She approached the hole. "Take me, Lord, take me instead." She fell to the grass, laid on her stomach, and reached for the oak box – kicking and screaming.

"Mama!" Kelly screamed. Carl snatched her hand. The assistant pastor picked Mama up from the ground with one hand. The daughters of the church hugged her and pulled her toward the automobiles. She put her head on Sister Agnes's chest as they walked. Several guests threw dirt in the opening. Some said their own personal prayer before leaving while others stood frozen in disbelief.

Carl walked behind the crowd with Kelly and me. She was too scared of Mama to go with her. I did not mind being with Carl, he seemed composed. The ride home was relaxing, so I sang myself to sleep. Once Kelly closed her eyes, it was time to get out the vehicle. There were visitors waiting on us when we arrived. Some held casserole dishes, paper products and sodas in their hands. Others sat in their cars chatting. I did not even know if some of them made it to the gravesite. *They look hungry and impatient.*

Sister Agnes and the other daughters helped Mama get everything ready. She opened the front door for us when we approached. The overwhelming scent of sweet potato pie made someone's belly growl. Once inside, everyone could smell all sorts of fragrances. The ribs, in particular, were second loudest in the room.

Mama appeared cooler, even Kelly noticed it. "Mama!" Kelly hugged her leg. Carl kissed her and she received him with a little passion.

30

"Awe, that's nice," someone remarked.

Mama blushed. "Come on in, everyone. Come on in. There is a lot to eat and I do not want any leftovers," she informed them. The group filed in as fast as they could – young and old.

Carl sat me in the bed until he could get himself together. I ogled at the ceiling. I heard chatter and soft music playing in the background. Carl returned in ten minutes to get me. I felt as though I could now count on him.

€€€

"It was a wonderful service. Mildred was a wonderful woman." A stranger hugged Mama and headed to the living room to get in the buffet line. Mama sucked her teeth and went back into the kitchen. She borrowed three rectangle banquet tables from the church and had them lined up along the wall in the living room. She and Carl cooked all night, mainly meats. Their friends brought some of the side dishes and desserts. I sat on Carl's lap, looking at all the food that passed before my eyes. One woman had turkey, cornbread dressing and greens. Her sidekick had ham, macaroni and cheese, green beans and cornbread.

Carl bounced his leg up and down, making me nauseous. If I spit up, maybe he would stop. Milk poured from my mouth.

"Yak, Dana. You almost got my new pants." He used the stained bib to rub my mouth.

Very smart, old dude.

The room filled with visitors, most I had never seen before and neither had Mama. Aunt Mildred did not have any kids, but she had been married five times. Husband number five showed up, the others sent their condolences.

Mama was estranged from her youngest two siblings since the death of their parents. They did not want to accept the fact that she received the house in their parents' will. All they received was money. They blew it within three months and asked Mama for some. When she refused, they stopped speaking to her. To this day, no one knew why Mama made out like a bandit when her parents died. The family rumored that she was the prettiest, but she found the explanation absurd. Now, she lives a debt-free life at the age of twenty-five.

Kelly played with the other little children in her bedroom. Occasionally, they would come out the room and run underneath folk's legs until someone yelled at them. The older kids were supposed to supervise them, but they were too busy playing video games and listening to music on cassette tapes.

Pastor Cherry left last because he did not want to depart without his check. Lucky for Mama, Aunt Mildred left her an insurance policy; otherwise, she would have cremated her or put her in a pine box. She was holding up well considering. Aunt Mildred was five years older than Mama and she looked up to her. I tried not to make waves since I knew that she needed some rest. She talked about getting some peace and quiet for the next few days. The house had been busy since Aunt Mildred died. Carl cleaned the kitchen and the living room, along with Bonnie. He did not want to seem like a total deadbeat even though everyone knew. They assumed that he laid the pipe really well – the only thing going for him at the age of thirty-five.

"Here you go, pastor." My mama handed him an envelope.

"Thank you. I better get going," He told her.

33

"Alright, pastor, I'll see you on Sunday," she responded.

He hugged her and Carl.

"See you Sunday, Carl?"

"Well…ah…I have to watch the kids."

"Okay, perhaps next time."

What! Carl lying to the pastor? That's just wrong. Wrong. Wrong. Wrong. Even I know better than to lie.

They walked him to the door. "Good night," they said in unison as they watched him get into his car.

"Watching the kids? Since when?" Mama asked, but not wanting an answer.

He moved his shoulders upward.

"Babysitting my ass, and lying to the pastor? Come on now."

She picked me up out of the playpen and headed to the bathroom for a bath. Kelly fell asleep two hours earlier on the loveseat, and Mama let her rest. I heard her say that she would give her a bath in the morning. Carl flopped down on the sofa, and then turned the volume up on the television. He mumbled something, but Mama ignored him.

"Mm… mm…mm."

I could not believe Mama was humming. She seemed to be in a good mood all of sudden, considering that she just buried her favorite sister. That was something I had never seen since I arrived on this earth almost eight weeks ago. Perhaps bath time made her as happy as me. All I had to do was sit in my baby tub and someone sponged water all over my legs, belly, and arms.

"Mm…mm…mm, here you go, baby." She sat me in the lukewarm water.

Awww! I feel good already.

Splash! Kick! Splatter!

Wait a minute…it…it is getting hotter.

"Mm…mm...mm." Mama sang louder and the water kept getting hotter. Her eyes looked glassy as she stared in the mirror.

"Www…um…waaa! Waaa!" *Please, Mama, stop! Stop!* I learned that crying meant there was a problem. Why wouldn't she stop?

I kicked my legs fast, hoping to knock the water off. Better yet, I wished it would hit her face, and then perhaps she would come to her senses. I slid my back downward, pushing water forward and onto the floor. That did not help, so I let out a piercing sound, thinking it would annoy her enough to stop. She picked me up and wrapped me in a towel. I smelled a mixture of vanilla lotion and sour beer. I wiggled my head to get the stink out my nose. She pressed my head in the middle of her chest again and patted my back. It stung because of the moisture and the heat from the water. I continued to whimper.

Thump! Thump! Thump! Her hits became more intense. I knew that I needed to calm down.

Thump! I felt the wind escape me with that one. Mama thought I stopped weeping, so she stopped.

Slurp! The slimy green stuff glided back into my nose and I regained my breath. No other noise came out. I breathed deeply until my heart resumed a normal beat.

What has gotten into mama? What did I do to deserve this?

€€€

The next day, I screamed every time that I passed the bathroom, especially after having two consecutive nightmares during the night. I dreamt that I went swimming in the tub, but I had to fight off two sharks. I kicked my legs faster in order to get away. It did not help, I still could not move. They gobbled me up. The second one repeated the first, but without any editing – very vivid mutilation. It terrified me. I did not know what to expect and I did not want to find out. I got excited when I learned that Carl was going to give me a bath. Mama had to complete a project for work, so she locked herself in her home office.

When Carl took me in there, Kelly had already gotten into the tub. She splashed water all over the place as she used her floatable book as a boat for her miniature dolls. I knew if something went wrong, she would save me. Therefore, I was back to my happy self at bath time.

Carl used the lavender bath gel on me. It smelled so good and calming, and it made me sleepy…sleepy…sleepy. I drifted off with the smiling angels. I was at peace on my cotton ball beanbag. I think it was time to pee, I felt it. *Come on…you can do it…you can do it*. It would not come. Why wouldn't it come out? I was hurting. It hurt badly. I might have to whimper to get somebody to check on this because it was not right. Carl should be able to help me. Let me at least open my right eye.

Carl? Carl? What are you doing to me, Carl?

"Waaa! Waa!"

"What's wrong, baby?" Kelly asked. She got out the tub to come see why I was crying.

Before she could get there, Carl released my clitoris. He had been squeezing it.

She put her step stool underneath the sink and climbed up to see over the basin where my tub sat. She looked at me with her brown eyes and did not see what the fuss was about. Carl appeared perturbed with her. She reached for the sponge and started bathing me. She did a good job, considering her age. She watched Carl finish and put on my robe. It was almost as if she knew and she wanted to protect me. Then, it dawned on me that she loved me unconditionally – unlike the others in the house. Kelly and I would always share a special bond that day forward.

€€€

Carl and Mama were in the other room arguing over who should give us a bath. They thought we could not hear them, but we could, even over the sound of Kelly talking to herself, the TV screaming at us, and the neighbor's barking dog.

"…I'm just saying, I think the mother should give her girls a bath."

"Why, Carl? Why you think that now? You have been giving them baths."

"Look, I did not sign up to do any of this, they are your kids."

"Thanks for the reminder."

There was silence for a moment. Next, I heard the front door slam.

"Okay, girls, let's get cleaned up," Mama ordered. I did not know if that was a good thing or bad. I guess I would soon find out.

€€€

Three months passed and Mama continued to wash us. She had not done anything crazy, lucky for me. I finally stopped whining when I was near or in the bathroom. Carl still refused to interact with us unless he had to, which made Mama handle her responsibilities. She did a decent job when she felt like it. Thus far, I was at peace.

Chapter 3

My skin darkened as I got older like Mama said. Though my hair thickened, it lost some of its elasticity. I wore it in an afro.

"You going to church today, Tracey?" Carl asked.

"Yes."

"You taking Dana this time?"

"No."

"Why not? The poor child has not seen the inside of a church in eight months."

"I do not want to."

"Why not?"

Mama stopped in the middle of the floor and gave him the evil eye. "We go through this almost every week."

"I know, but perhaps I have something to do today."

"You have somewhere to go, Carl?"

"Well…um…no."

"Okay. Watch Dana."

"Can't you at least wash and comb her hair? I am sick of looking at it. It looks filthy and matted."

40

"I will when I return." She made sure she switched her hips while leaving the room.

Yeah right. She had not washed my hair since the day before Aunt Mildred's funeral. I scratched my head every day. The dry and brittle pieces fell out on a regular basis. Mama oiled it once a week, but she used my nappy head as an excuse for not taking me to church. Every time they returned, Kelly showed me her pictures, projects or goodies. I dribbled on them, but Kelly did not complain. She diverted her attention to something else more important. I wanted to go with her sometime so that I could get my own stuff.

"Pastor Cherry asked about you today," Mama told Carl.

"Oh yeah, what did you say?"

"You stayed home to babysit Dana."

"Um."

"Then, he gave me a lecture about not bringing ya'll."

"Good."

"Good nothing. Both of you are going next week, so be prepared."

"What?"

Mama shook her head. I did it, too, and then laughed at her.

€€€

I cried as the suds ran down my face.

"What's wrong, baby? Oh, you have soap in your eyes?" Mama moved her hand across my face. "Perhaps I can rub some of that ugly off of you."

Yes, hurry, Mama, get them out. I cannot see. She is sure taking her sweet time. She leaned me underneath the faucet and let the water pour over my face. I hit the metal contraption when I tried to escape the liquid and that made me cry.

"Stop moving, Dana, stop."

I moved my hands and body too fast for Mama. Water flowed into my nose and mouth. *I am drowning. Forget this hair washing thing. I hate it.*

Mama removed me from the sink and placed a towel over my head. Then, she lifted it up. "Peek-a-boo." She repeated it and it made me feel a little better. The last time she covered me, she left it there. I could not see a thing. I remained still.

I started crying. Someone was pressing the towel into my nose and mouth. It moved. I saw Mama.

She balled it up, then pushed it in my face. I cried again. What was happening? I could not…I could not…breathe. I coughed and cried.

"Mama, can I have something to drink?" Kelly wanted to know. She let the towel drop. "Peek-a-boo, Dana," she played it off.

I cried and coughed more. *This bitch is crazy.*

"I want to play with Dana, Mama."

"No, I'll get your Kool-Aid."

Kelly smiled at me while I finished my tantrum.

"Here. What you say?"

"Thank you, Mama."

Thank you Kelly. Always on the scene in the nick of time.

Mama dried me off like she was supposed to and took me into the living room. She dug in her cosmetic bag for a fine-tooth comb and picked my hair.

I started crying.

"Shut up, baby," Mama advised. "It will be okay."

The more I cried, the faster she raked. Sometimes, the comb's teeth stuck in my bush. She yanked on it until it flew out, making me cry harder.

€€€

After spending all morning getting my locks in order for church, as soon as we arrived, I caught a little snooze. When I woke up, I rolled over in a bed and sat up. I looked around the room, but I did not see anyone. Toys covered most of the floor, artwork dangled from the ceilings and the chairs lined up against the wall. I did not know how I got there or how long I had been there. The last thing that I remembered was seeing Pastor Cherry approach Mama. Sister Agnes was busy having a conversation with Kelly and some other little girls across the room. I had no recollection about Carl's whereabouts. No one had seen him since the day before. That might explain why I had to suffer earlier.

"Ma, ma, ma," I chanted, hoping someone would hear me. I said it louder. Still nothing. I tried pulling myself up. I grasped the bars and jerked my shoulders. Success. I stood and said it again, but with little more whine with it. "Ma! Ma! Ma!" No one came. I fell down, derrière first, then collapsed backward. I lie there imagining taking a ride on the paper mâché airplane. It could take me to a faraway place above the clouds.

I blew bubbles and sang. When the air conditioner cranked up, the aircraft moved back and forth. I watched it, hoping it would not leave my sight. I was comfortable, though a bit hungry. I did not see anything that resembled food or milk. *That red sure does look pretty.* I began farting up a storm. The rumble crept up my back. I found it humorous, making my tummy wiggle when I chuckled. I was enjoying being detached.

Boom! I jumped and turned toward the noise. *Carl. Pastor Cherry.*

"There she is," Carl spouted.

"Oh, thank God. I am sorry. I will get to the bottom of this tomorrow. This is unacceptable."

"No problem, Pastor. It is not your fault. Tracey should have remembered to get her."

"Thank you. But, don't be so hard on Tracey. I am glad Miss Dana is unharmed. Plus, we got you to come to church today."

"Right," Carl responded in an uneasy laugh. He embraced and kissed me. I tried to grab my visual friend, but I was not tall enough in Carl's arm to reach it.

"I see you later, Pastor."

"I am going to hold you to it."

Carl sneered. He trotted out as fast as he could before the pastor said something else. When we got outside, I could see the sunset. The oranges, reds, and yellows complemented each other. A thin, white light encircled it, reminding me of the day I saw Aunt Mildred. I waved. Carl gave me a high-five and buckled me into my seat.

€€€

"Dana!" Kelly greeted me at the door. I got excited thinking about her playing with me, however, she walked away instead. Mama chilled on the couch as if nothing happened. Carl sat in the recliner with me on his lap.

"Now, tell me again how you forgot the baby?" he asked Mama. I sat quietly so that I could hear the answer, too, even though I considered the time alone bittersweet. I rested my head on Carl's abdomen.

"Carl, I am trying to watch my program. We went over this already," Mama stated.

"And, what I cannot understand is why the Sunday School providers left her in there. Pastor Cherry

46

needs to fire them."

"You are overreacting."

"Are you kidding me? What if I did not come back tonight Tracey?"

Mama resumed gawking at a true crime story. Carl rubbed his head in frustration.

"I cannot take this anymore," he murmured.

The flashing lights coming from the tube mesmerized me. It did not take me long to move on with my life.

Chapter 4

"Bay, I just realized that tomorrow is Dana's birthday." I heard my name, so I stood up in my playpen.

"Really?"

"Yes, what are we doing?"

"What do you mean?"

"What do you mean, what I mean? Your baby turns one year old tomorrow. How are we going to celebrate?"

"We are not."

"Come on, Tracey. You have to do something for the kid."

"You got your nerve."

"Whew, you right."

He patted his face. I mocked him. He cackled. Kelly decided to join in, too. Mama could not stand the sound. She increased the volume on the television. Everyone resumed their previous activities. I gummed a brown teddy bear. Fuzzy stuff got in my mouth. I swallowed them and continued for more. Kelly combed her Barbie head. Occasionally, she got into an argument with the plastic beauty.

€€€

"Happy birthday, Dana," Carl sang. He gave me a huge hug and several kisses. "If I had some money, you would have a blast today," he whispered.

Mama did not work. I guess she wanted to spend it with me, but she had not gotten out of bed. Normally, she was awake by now.

Carl carried me around the house in a baby sling while he cooked and cleaned. I think Mama bought it for him as a joke, but he decided to use it. I guess the joke was on her. I did not see Mama anywhere. Carl put on my clothes – a jean skirt, pink polo, white bobby socks and knock off Adidas sneakers.

"Dang, this outfit is tight." He tried another, then another. He chose a t-shirt, but it was too small as well.

"You need some new clothes, baby girl."

"Carl. Carl. Where are you?" Mama called.

"In Dana's room!" he bellowed, nearly scaring me to death.

She made a grand entrance. "Oh, hay, honey." They kissed.

"I am trying to find something for Dana to wear. It's her birthday."

"I know. I know." She thumped his chest two times with her right hand.

"You have something in that bag?"

"Not for Dana." She dumped the contents in the bag onto the bed. She admired the three dresses, six pairs of socks, and two sets of pajamas.

"Who is that for?"

"Kelly."

"Why are you buying Kelly something on Dana's birthday? She needed a few items, plus, she has been a good girl."

"Did I miss something here?" Carl wondered.

Mama kissed my cheek. "Happy birthday, Dana."

"Ma. Ma. Ma." I thought she was going to hold me, but instead, she ignored me. "Ma. Ma. Ma."

"I have to go wake Kelly, she needs to try on her new duds."

Carl walked over to the bedroom window so that I could view the scenery. I saw green leaves on the oak trees and birds flying around them. When I got older, I planned to claim them. My attention moved to the dog running down the sidewalk chasing a squirrel. Even animals found fun in their daily lives. I would run with them someday. If I got away, though, I may run free.

"Uncle Carl, look. Look what mama brought me." Kelly swung her hip side-to-side so he could get the full effect.

"How nice, Kelly. You look beautiful."

"What do you say, Kelly?" Mama solicited.

"Thank you." She returned to her room.

"Did you at least purchase a cake for Dana?"

"This conversation is over, Carl."

"Here. Take your daughter. I am going out." He pressed me into her chest. I liked that game. I viewed Mama's face with pleasure, but she did not reply the same way. She threw me on the bed. I bounced once, hopped up, and landed face up on the floor. I cried and called her name.

"Dana!" Mama screamed, ran to my rescue and caressed me in her arms. "I am sorry. I am so sorry." She rocked forward, then back. Kelly saw Mama on the floor.

"What's wrong, Mama? She shook her shoulder. "What's wrong?" Mama did not say anything. Kelly eased to the ground, laid her head on Mama's arm, and motioned with her.

I fell asleep. Everything turned white, then it faded into hazy images. I thought I saw Aunt Mildred. She was having a conversation with someone. I reached for her, but a window blocked me from touching her. I knocked on it to get her attention. When she saw me, I waved. She stared at me for a minute, then she cried. Shadowy figures surrounded and comforted her. However, I saw her clearly.

"My darling, Dana. I love you and I miss you. I will always be with you and protect you, all you have to do is believe," she said.

"Okay, Auntie. Okay." I squeezed my eyes and woke up coughing.

"Dana, wake up." I heard Mama say.

She sat me up to catch my breath as I continued to cough.

"That's it, baby, breathe."

I resumed my jovial self and that made Mama feel at ease. She climbed into the rocking chair with the both of us and read a picture book, *Sweet Potato Pie*. I was grateful for my birthday gift, I got to live another day.

€€€

Now that I was one, I could eat table food like the other tots that I observed on TV. Those delicious looking meals would be mine and I could not wait. I wondered when Mama would let me try them. After all, it was almost dinnertime. I would beg, grab, and whine until I got what I wanted. I saw Kelly. "Um…um…um," I sang.

"Mama, Dana is hungry. She wants some of my food," Kelly yelled. She served me a spoonful of mashed potatoes.

"Um. Smack. Um. Smack." *I want more.*   Kelly noticed and shoved some in my mouth. *Faster, Kelly, faster*. She kept putting it in until nothing remained.

"Awe. I'm telling Mama."

I looked at her as if she lost her mind. Where was she going with that plate? I scooted my walker toward the kitchen, but the doggone coffee table blocked the way. I began to cry.

Kelly returned with Mama. They both had a dish. *Hurray, more for me.* Kelly started to give me more when Mama knocked her spoon out her hand.

"Didn't I tell you not to feed that baby?" Kelly tilted her head down. "Go sit over there and eat your food."

I began crying. *Someone, anyone, please give me something to eat.* I got louder and moved closer to Mama, who sat on the couch. She pushed me away with her foot and I slid in front of the television.

"Move, Dana, move. You are in the way. Mama, Dana won't move. I cannot see *Dora, the Explorer,*" Kelly whined. I stopped fussing for a minute and watched her eat. "Move I said."

Here she comes. She kicked my leg and I started crying. "Why did you do that?" Mama asked.

"Because she would not move."

"Next time, use your hands and get her out the way. She still doesn't understand you."

Kelly scraped her plate and went to the kitchen to get seconds. Mama sucked down vittles, too. I sat in the corner whimpering like a puppy while watching them eat.

€€€

It was a new day, and I was hoping to get some solid food. All I had the night before was formula. I did not even get an upgrade on my milk. Carl did not say anything to Mama because he did not know any better, he just inserted bottle. He watched me during the day while Mama worked. He followed the written schedule that hung on the refrigerator; even the diaper changes were planned. It worked well for everyone. Kelly had a different babysitter. Mama took her to pre-school in the morning and the neighbor retrieved her in the afternoon until Mama got home.

I ate, slept and played by myself. Carl did not interact with me unless he had a reason, nor did he give me baths. I guess I should not complain. Mama bathed me at night as well as selected my clothes.

I get to sit in the highchair across from my sister. Alright! The aroma from the spaghetti sauce made me drool. I was close enough to the kitchen table to reach someone or something.

"Dinner," Mama chimed.

Carl came in holding Kelly. "Yeah, sketti," she added. He sat her down and fixed his place.

"Okay, dig in," Mama told us. However, all I had was a bottle sitting in front of me. I threw it on the floor and Carl placed it back. I did it again. Mama flung it and it slid on the tray. I got ready to do it again. She held up her hand as if she planned to hit me. I blinked my eyes rapidly, hoping that she did not. I decided to leave it alone.

"Let her try the spaghetti," Carl commented. She sighed.

"Okay, smarty pants." She forced her fork in my mouth.

"Oh," I moaned. I stuck out my tongue and the food fell. I did not know what was worse, the fork stabbing me or the heat from the food piercing my tongue. I licked the tangy substance on lips. "Um."

"It is probably too hot, Tracey."

"Oh, no it is not."

"Well, mine is."

Mama repeated her steps, and I cried and moved my head. *I change my mind. I do not want spaghetti tonight.* I scooped up my milk instead. Mama snatched it out my hand and moved it to the counter out of my reach. I opened my mouth and cried, and she threw food inside. I made sure not to open up again. She put the fork to my lips, anyway. I held them shut. When I did not release them, she thrusts it on my lips, making me cry. "Tracey, you are mean as hell. I cannot watch this," Carl said and took his meal into the other room. I guess she felt some compassion and returned my drink to me. Though it tasted spoiled, I felt comfort knowing that I had it in my mouth instead of that red stuff.

€€€

Mama got me up early the next morning to feed me since Carl's hangover had him moving slow. He stayed out late the night before with the boys. I figured I would get oatmeal or cereal. When we get to the kitchen, I noticed Kelly eating oatmeal with consecutive scoops. If I could talk, I would ask her for some. "Um. Um."

"You like the sight of that, don't you, Dana?" Mama teased.

"Ma, ma, ma," I chanted.

I sat patiently as she served up a heaping in bowl. "Open up, Dana." I did as wide as I could.

I cried and spit the hot food in Mama's face. She reacted by slapping my lips. The noise scared Kelly.

"Mama, what's wrong with Dana?"

"Nothing, baby. Go get your things so that we can go." Kelly approached me and put her hands over my mouth to muffle the sound, but that didn't stop me from crying.

"You are a funny girl." Mama removed her hands from my face as she laughed. "Go on." Kelly rolled her neck and left.

"What's wrong with her now, Tracey?" Carl asked perturbed.

"I don't know. She is yours. I have to go to work."

I hated food. I did not want to eat anything else. Right on cue, Carl put the bottle in my mouth. I got the next feeding in four hours.

€€€

"What shall I do, doctor? Dana will not eat."

"Miss Calhoun, I suggest giving her two percent milk and put cereal in it. Also, purchase some Insure so that we can get her weight up. Try introducing soft items such as beans, peas, noodles, and potatoes. Make the food accessible so that when she gets hungry, she can eat."

I sat there listening to the man with the baritone voice as if I knew what he was talking about. I figured it was about me, but who cared, he looked cute with the silvery things in his pocket.

"Okay, doctor, I get it. What if none of this works?"

"Bring her back in, I'll run some tests. I would not worry about anything yet."

"Yet?"

"Right, otherwise, I will have to investigate you for neglecting your baby." The doctor laughed. "Just kidding Miss Calhoun."

I laughed, too. He smiled back.

Mama did not find us amazing. She seemed a little nervous and gathered her items. "I better get going, doctor." She cut our fun short.

"Okay, have a nice day, Dana."

I grinned again. "Coo. A-coo." He tickled my belly and Mama swung me away from him.

He regained his professionalism. "Have a good day, Miss Calhoun."

"Bye."

I felt good, even though my empty stomach growled. The gurgles remind me of a foreign language. I swung my legs and sang in the backseat. Mama pulled into a chicken fast food joint and I breathed in the grease. It reminded me of the bacon that mama cooked for breakfast sometimes.

"Yes, I like a small potatoes and gravy, and a number three with macaroni and cheese."

I hope she buys me something. When we got home, Mama fed me the potatoes and gravy. "Yum. Yum." *I love them! They taste wonderful on my lips and going down my throat. They are the right temperature. I want more, and more, and more.* "Yum! Yum! Yum!"

"See, I knew she would eat potatoes," Carl commented with pride. Mama glared at him and rolled her eyes. Kelly stood nearby to watch while she tugged the skin on her chicken.

Chapter 5

My hair grew thicker and longer over the next year since Mama started washing and styling it on a regular basis. I still disliked her touching it. I sensed the pain before she began her approach. I looked forward to the day when I could do it myself.

"Oh…" I grunted, trying to reach the brush. If I stood on my tiptoes, I could get it off Mama's dresser. "Got it." I ran it through my head, and sometimes accidentally hit my eyelashes. "Ouch." I laughed.

"Dana." Mama grabbed the tool out my hand and threw it on the highboy. "Come on, time to eat." I ran behind her to the kitchen. I sat in my chair and waited for her to deliver my plate. My vocabulary grew each day. "Eat! Eat! Eat!" She dropped the dish down, agitated with my racket.

"I am so glad you are getting older, Dana. Pretty soon, you will be an independent little person," Mama told me while I ate my eggs and sausage links. I had an appetite and I had picked up some weight. According to some folks, I was still on the skinny side. I did not mind, I planned to eat everything in sight. I did not discriminate.

Mama requested the day off because it was Kelly's first day at all-day kindergarten. She packed Kelly's backpack with school supplies and a lunch.

"Kelly, are you ready?"

"Yes." She strolled in with her white shirt, plaid skirt, and black and white Mary Jane shoes.

"Oh, Kelly, you've been playing in your hair again?" Mama rushed out the room and returned with the comb. Kelly snuck one of my links.

"Stop!" I yelled.

"Get over here so that I can straighten this hair back like I had it. Stop playing in it. Do you hear me?"

Kelly nodded.

"I cannot hear you."

"Yes."

"And, make sure you say yes ma'am to your teacher. Okay?"

She moved her head slightly, "Yes."

"Alright. Let's go."

€€€

The school's walkway consisted of parents with digital cameras and video recorders – look out, Hollywood. It was like a party. Mama did not have her equipment, but she had big smiles and love for her daughter.

"Hi," I said to every person that I passed.

"Are you nervous, Kelly?" Mama inquired.

She did not speak. Mama found the classroom and introduced herself to the teacher. I ran off to play with the blocks by the window. Kelly held Mama's hand tight. As soon as I put the blue block on top of the green one, Mama pulled my arm in her direction. Kelly found a seat between a boy named Murray and a girl named Piper. We waited awhile to ensure Kelly would be all right. Mama observed the other students and the teacher. She admired the bulletin boards while I gravitated to the different shapes on the poster board.

"Well, Kelly, we better get going. Say goodbye to your sister."

"Bye, Dana. See you when I get home."

"Ewe, that's your sister?" Murray asked.

"Yes."

"What's wrong with her face?" Piper asked.

"Nothing."

"Her hair does not look like yours."

"I know."

"Yours is pretty." Piper ran her finger through Kelly's hair.

"Yeah," Murray concurred.

Mama kissed Kelly and departed. She did not say anything to the teacher. She trotted so fast that I lagged behind, even with her clutching my hand. Before we drove away from the school, Mama turned around to check on me in the backseat. She headed to the beauty supply store. She left me in the car with it running and the doors unlocked. I viewed people passing by on their busy schedule. Most did not notice that I was in there. However, one person did. The thin man standing in front of the barbershop studied me. I glanced at him in between the other distractions. He threw his cigarette down and walked closer. The nearer he got, the scarier his face appeared. It was pink with red craters and wrinkles on his forehead. His black hair with gray streaks fell into his face. He pushed the bang to the side with his left hand and reached for the door with his right.

Mama jumped into the car. "I am back, Dana." She put the car in reverse without even noticing the guy near the door. She almost took his foot off as he stood there watching us speed off in the Toyota Camry.

When we arrived home, Mama rushed us into the house, opened her bag, and removed a square box with a little girl on the cover smiling. She sat me in my chair and parted my hair in four sections with a comb.

"Ouch. Ouch, Mama," I complained.

"It won't' be long now, Dana."

I had no idea what she was talking about or doing. She mixed a liquid substance with a white solution. Mama put on plastic gloves and scooped some into her hands. She plopped it onto my head, and the odor from the clear container made my eyes water. As she moved it over my hair, it tingled. I shook my head because I was ready to get out of the chair.

"Hold still, Dana."

"No."

"What?"

"No." I wobbled my head. Mama gripped it so that I stopped the motion. She did it with such force, I dared not move again. I sat there kicking my legs and humming. That did not bother Mama while she worked the relaxer on every strand. When she finished, she took me to the sink and pushed my skull under the faucet to rinse the goo out my hair. Then, she washed it with shampoo twice. She dropped me back into my chair and used a hand held blow dryer.

"Hot, Mama, hot."

"Dana, I am almost done. Please, sit still.

I pull on my hair. "Hot. Hot, Mama."

She slapped my legs. "Stop it, Dana."

"Ouch. Mama. Ouch."

"I know, but you must not make Mama mad."

I started crying.

"Okay, now you are faking it."

It did hurt, but I was being a little dramatic. I wanted out the chair so bad that I could scream.

"See how nice that feels?" Mama brushed my hair from the top to the bottom – about eighteen inches. Then, she held a mirror up to my face so that I could see. I was beautiful. My mane shined and it even bounced when I moved my head. I could not believe Mama did that for me. She brought the comb near my head and I shrugged my shoulder in anticipation for the pain.

"Wow, Dana." She scraped the instrument in and out of my head with ease. The strokes did not bother me. I loved it – no more pain.

It was a great day. I spent the rest of the morning and afternoon drawing, playing with my baby dolls, and napping. Mama watched her soap operas, and game and talk shows. I knew not to bother her. When I get a little fussy, she nipped it in the bud quickly by letting me snack on cheese puffs, mandarin oranges, or toddler cookies.

"Hey, Tracey," Carl greeted her.

"Hello, now be quiet. Maury is getting ready to announce if this guy is the father."

"Alrighty then."

I was too busy to say anything to Carl. He walked over to pinch my cheeks. I smacked his hands away, and he tried again and got me.

"Ouch, Carl."

"Dana, your hair. What happened?

I touched it and continued doing what I was doing.

"Hey, Tracey, what did you do to Dana's hair?"

"I relaxed it…he is the father." Mama cheered.

"You relaxed a two year old's hair?"

"Carl, why don't you take your sorry ass back where you were?"

"Don't worry, I will." He huffed while leaving the room.

"You know what, Dana? You need a trim. Your ends are out of control," Mama chimed. She left the room and returned with the sheers. "Come here, Dana."

I ignored her.

"Dana, come here."

I still did not move. I did not feel like it. *I do not hassle her, especially during her favorite activities. Why is she bothering me?*

"Come here now!"

I got tired of her bossing me. I walked over slowly and prepared myself for my punishment.

"Park it here." She pointed between her legs to the sofa.

Mama placed a towel around my shoulders and started cutting. "You don't need all this hair. It makes little black girls look funny."

"Funny, Mama."

"Yes, funny."

68

I laughed at Mama saying funny. She mimicked me. She cut some more until she whacked nine inches. I felt lighter. Good thing she got rid of those pesky split ends.

"There. You are ready for the world."

"Yes," I commented as if she asked me a question.

Mama dug in Kelly's hair pail for some accessories. She parted my hair down the middle of my head from front to back. Then, she parted it across. She put pink hairballs around two sections and a white one on the other two. She twisted each one and clasped matching barrettes on the ends. I wore a pink t-shirt, white shorts, white tennis shoes, and pink socks.

ЄЄЄ

"Look at your sister, Kelly." Piper pointed in our direction.

Kelly came running toward the car. "Mama!" She hugged her.

"Hi, Kelly. How was school?" Mama asked.

"Hi, Kelly," I repeated just because.

"Good. What happen to Dana's hair?"

"I gave her a relaxer."

69

"I like her four ponytails."

I swung them so that the barrettes at the bottom hit me in my face.

"They do look good, don't they?"

"Bye, Kelly, see you tomorrow," Murray yelled. "I like your sister's new hair."

Kelly waved at all her new friends with a gloomy face. "Mama, can I get new hair, too?"

"Bye." I waved at all the students, too, as if they were my friends.

"You are funny, Kelly. You do not need new hair, you already have good hair. Now, let's go home."

Kelly poked her lips out and whined while getting into the car.

"Enough, Kelly. I don't want to hear anymore."

"But, you said that I was pretty."

I did not recall Mama telling me that. She must have thought that folks admired my hair now.

"You are."

She surveyed my tresses and then tugged my plait.

"Ouch." I swung my hand at her.

"Mama, Dana is fighting me."

"Dana!" Mama peered at me in the rearview mirror.

"Stop," I told Kelly and waved my finger in her face.

Snap! She missed it, and bit the air instead.

"Don't have me pull this car over, you two."

Mama's expression screamed, "I mean business." I was not trying to get in trouble, especially with my perfect doo and my matching clothes.

When we arrived home, I unbuckled myself and exited before Kelly did. She contemplated on staying in the car until Mama gave her "the look." She dashed past me, almost knocking me down, to get to the door first. I was too busy trying to catch a black and yellow butterfly.

"Come on in here, Dana," Mama commanded.

I obeyed that time and headed directly to the kitchen. It should be time for a snack or dinner. It did not matter to me as long as someone gave me some food. Since I had tasted a variety of items, eating was a hobby for me.

"Kelly, I am tired of seeing the sad face. What is the problem?"

"I want new hair."

"You are still on that?"

"Yes."

"I will take care of it tomorrow, okay?" She hugged her first born while I ate McDonald's chicken nuggets. I had a piece in each hand and alternated my bites.

"Yum. Yum. Yum." I did not need any affection. I had to finish my food before it disappeared. "Yum. Yum. Yum." Carl did not want his food, he was hoping for a home cooked meal. He grumbled something and walked out the door. I guess I'd eat his fries. I reached for the white bag.

€€€

"Oh, Dana, look at your hair," Mama mentioned.

I touched it, but I had no clue what she was complaining about early in the morning. The only thing that mattered to me was banana, oatmeal, and milk. Carl fixed it for me at least twice a week.

"Her scarf must have come off while she was sleeping. You know the girl is a wild sleeper," Carl reminded her.

She leaned toward my face. I thought she may actually kiss me, so I puckered up my lips to get ready for it.

"I sure didn't get those edges too good. Carl, you will have to take careof it today, I don't have time." She walked away, leaving me hanging. I was not surprised that she did not show me any love. What was I thinking? Morning time really sucked.

"What are you talking about?" Carl asked.

"I have gel in my bathroom, put some around her temples." She massaged my scalp. "Take the hair moisturizer in the green bottle and put a little just above her scalp. It is still wavy in there. Then, put some on her actual hair all the way to the ends, moisture on the ends are very important. Repeat the process, it seems a little dry and brittle."

"That sounds like a lot of work. Why can't you do it when you get home?"

"I do every fucking thing around this house already. Why can't you do this one thing that I ask?"

"Hey, don't cuss at me like that. I watch your damn children all the time. Matter of fact, who keeps

73

Dana while your ass is working? Don't give me no shit."

"Carl? Carl? Where are you going?"

"I got things to do. Find you another babysitter."

"But, I have to work today."

I never heard Mama whine before, it was kind of nice to see her weak for a change.

Slam!

"Carl, wait! Carl, wait!" Mama pounded on the front door with her fist. "I would not have this damn problem if you had better hair," Mama yelled at me with her hands on her hips.

I decided to pull the dry cereal out the pantry and eat it. I sat on the ceramic tile with my legs folded and the box tipped over on the floor. Mama fed Kelly when she first woke up, so by the time I got up, Carl had to prepare my meal. One day, I hoped to rise with food already waiting for me.

Mama phoned several people to see if they could watch me. No one said yes, but they would have, had it been Kelly. She called the hospital to tell them that she needed a personal day. Her boss did not sound too happy about the request; I could hear loud chatter coming from the phone. Mama held the receiver inches from her face.

She cussed her boss when she slammed down the phone.

I cruised the Cheerios up and down the table leg while I chewed a mouthful.

"Mama, here, the box. I want to look like her?" Kelly held a kiddie relaxer.

"Kelly, give me that." She snatched it and threw it on the table. "Go get your things so that we can go."

"But, Mama," Kelly complained. "I want to look like her." Kelly did an "I am irritated" dance.

Mama ignored her.

"Come here." Mama's curled finger wagged while she looked at me.

I know she is not talking to me. I am eating and playing.

"Come here, Dana." She approached, lifted me off the ground, and dropped me in my chair. She did not give me time to pick-up my cereal.

"Awe no. Awe no." I squirmed in my seat, not knowing what that woman wanted to do with me.

Mama grabbed the box from the table and started doing the same things that she did the day before. I hoped I did not have to do that every day. It was getting on my nerves, but I adored my hair when she finished. The fumes seem stronger than last time. First, I squinted my eyes, then I blinked them repeatedly. The cool sensation got warm fast. I move my head side-to-side, hoping to shake it loose. Mama moved my hands out the way because I kept trying to get it out my head.

"Move your hand, Dana."

I started crying. "Mama. No. Stop," I told her.

"Mama, what's wrong with Dana?" Kelly picked up the box. "She gets new hair again? Mama. Mama!"

"Shut up, Kelly. Shut the hell up."

Mama rushed me to the sink to rinse the bad stuff off my head. I screamed louder when she ran the cold water over it. My hair started coming out in chunks, some getting caught between her fingers. The only thing that mattered was relieving the pain that penetrated my skull. She washed out the remaining neutralizer shampoo and then conditioning shampoo.

She dried my hair with the towel and I trembled from the dampness because she didn't use the hairdryer that time. She held the mirror up so that I could look.

"See what you made me do?"

I focused my watery eyes. I had patches of hair missing in some places while the longer pieces hung on for life. Kelly peeped into the kitchen and laughed. She ran out because she could not bear my screaming. Mama retrieved a baseball cap from her room and placed it on my head. She did not want the kids at Kelly's school to see my hair now. I cried without sound all the way there.

Mama got out the car without me that time. *I guess she is too embarrassed to be seen with me.* She did not go far. I could see her talking to Kelly's teacher. Murray and Piper glanced inside the car and I waved to them. They did not recognize me, so they did not respond.

"I saw your brother," Murray told Kelly.

"That's Dana," she explained.

"Let's go play." Piper grabbed Kelly's hand, then Murray's. The three of them ran into the building together.

Mama smiled at the teacher, said goodbye, then scuttled back to the car. I was almost in sleepyville. I sang *The Itsy Bitsy Spider*." No one could comprehend what I was saying because I was mumbling. Mama's face showed no amazement. She sped away from the curb and I fell asleep before she made it to the corner.

When we returned home, Mama used Carl's clippers to cut my hair. When she finished, it resembled a boy's fade cut. Then, she poured Aloe Vera juice on my head to soothe the burn spots on my scalp. It felt better, however, I spent the entire afternoon whining and taking catnaps. When I woke, she rubbed petroleum jelly on my scalp. I sat there like a big girl and let her. I was too pooped to resist.

"What happened to her head?" Carl asked when he entered the living room.

Mama rolled her eyes at him. "Where have you been?"

"I went to get some breakfast and I stopped by my mother's house."

"Um."

He sat down next to us and glided his hand across my head. I wanted to impede him, but I did not have any energy.

"She looks like a little boy now."

"I know. I know. Bad perm. If I take care of it, it will grow back nicely."

"Yeah, but I know that it will never be the same."

She shook her head in agreement. I nodded mine as well. She pushed me away from her when she completed her task and I stood next to the couch staring at her for no reason other than being tired. Her and Carl hugged and kissed each other. *I guess they are making up.*

"Oh, Carl, stop. I don't have much time. I have to go get Kelly."

He nibbled on her ear. "We have enough time. Come on, baby."

"What are you looking at?" Mama asked me. She picked up the remote and turned on Sponge Bob. I observed the volume counter escalating to twenty. Then, she went to her room and Carl followed behind like a puppy dog. I maneuvered myself onto the sofa and lifted up the Barbie doll that was wedged in between the cushions. I placed her on my lap and ran my fingers through her blond hair. The long locks reminded me of mine. I touched my head and cry internally.

Chapter 6

"What the hell is going in here? Carl?" Mama slapped his back with a wide hand. "Get your ass up!" Carl jumped up dazed and confused. Kelly and I laughed hysterically as we watched the drama unfold.

"Who in the hell is this bitch and why is she in my house!" Mama hopped on the bed with her high heels and reached for the woman's hair. Carl tried to get to her before she put her hands on Bonnie's sister, Angel, but he stumbled on the sheets and fell face down on the bed.

"Ouch, bitch! Who the hell are you?" Angel responded angrily.

Mama slapped her. "I don't have to say shit to you. Get the fuck out my bed!" The woman tumbled to the floor and snatched her clothes.

"That nigga told me this was his house."

"His house? His house? I'll show him who house this is." She picked up the lamp on the nightstand and tossed it against the wall.

"Calm down, baby."

"You better get the hell out of here before I get my gat."

"What?" Carl and his mistress responded in unison.

"Awww, hell… we better get the hell up out of here because she means it."

They picked up some of their clothing and ran toward the front door. The woman pushed Carl out the way so that she could exit first. He shifted to the right, bumping into the couch.

The screen door almost broke when it slammed.

Mama searched her closet for her weapon to no avail. Kelly and I stood in the doorway as Carl and his lady friend jogged down Appian Way. *That's what he gets for being a bum and cheating on my mama.*

Our insidious laughter made my mama start laughing and crying at the same time. She dropped down on her knees and put her hands on her face, trying to cover up the embarrassment. Kelly and I comforted her.

"It's going to be okay, Mama," Kelly told her and touched her back.

"It's going to be okay, Mama," I reminded her, doing the same thing. Mama moved her shoulder as if I had cooties and reached out for Kelly. They shared a hug for three minutes as I watched. I experienced a sense of emptiness as always, and I was only five years old.

I felt as though the last three years flew by so fast. Mama kept her promise about taking care of my hair. She styled and moisturized it daily, and washed and deep conditioned it every Sunday evening. She trimmed the ends once a month – no more of that psycho cutting or relaxers. She no longer used any heat on it. As a result, it had grown two inches per year.

Mama still did not celebrate my birthday, but she made it a point to get Kelly something on my special day. I could not figure that one out, perhaps I would once I got older. In addition, Mama purchased Kelly gifts when she felt like it. I asked for things all the time, but I did not get them. I was used to it, though. If I looked like Kelly, she would do it for me.

€€€

When we arrived home from school the next day, Carl was sitting on the front porch.

"I don't have any where to go, Tracey."

She walked past him and pushed the back of his head forward.

"Come on in the house, children. You too, stupid ass."

Here he comes, back into our lives again. He assumed a passive role right away and stayed around the house because he needed a place to live and someone to take care of him. Even though Mama worked with professional men all day, she still gravitated to the scum of the earth. She made a living as a pharmacist at the largest hospital in the state, Buchanan General, and graduated from Xavier University with honors. None of her friends would dare tell her that Carl was all wrong for her. She loved him.

€€€

"Be still, Dana. How am I supposed to do your hair and you keep moving?"

"It hurts! It hurts! You are pulling too hard."

"Then, hold still."

Mama pulled the comb upward, sometimes doing it deliberately.

"Ouch! Ouch! Please, hurry. Please!"

"Be a big girl."

I held my head stiff as best I could for the next ten minutes. I was tortured every time that I got my hair braided. I had much rather wear ponytails. Kelly did not have to worry about hers for two reasons. One, she knew how to do her own hair. Two, she could manage her soft hair. She was born that way – nice locks, thin nose, and curvy, even at her age. I, on the other hand, had course hair, a large nose, and skinny. Also, I was darker than my sister. I guess having different fathers had something to do with it.

My mama never talked about my dad, but she dragged on and on about Kelly's father, Dino Nguyen from the Philippines. She told Kelly and me the stories about how they met in college, and how they had planned to get married and have children. Dino was deported before he could propose to Mama. Two weeks later, Mama learned that she was pregnant with Kelly. He wrote to her throughout her pregnancy with promises of returning to the states. He sent gifts and money after Kelly's birth while Mama mailed him pictures periodically. After Kelly's second birthday, he stopped corresponding with Mama. She had not heard from him since. Some of his old friends say that he was an aspiring rapper living in Las Vegas. I do not know why Mama told me those stories. I could care less.

"My daddy looks better than your daddy." Kelly waved a black and white photo in front of my face.

"So," I responded, and then tried to take away the picture. Kelly moved her hands in circle. I could not seize it. I jumped up and down in the air and she laughed at me.

"You don't know your daddy," she taunted.

"So."

"Who's your daddy? Who's your daddy?" Kelly pumped her pelvic upward in the air as she chanted.

"So what. I don't need no daddy."

"Is so all you have to say?"

"Yeah!"

I went into Mama's bedroom to tell her what Kelly had done to me.

"Mama, Kelly making fun of my daddy."

"Move from in front of the television, Dana."

"Ma, did you hear me? Kelly…"

"I heard you, move out the way. Kelly, stop!"

Though Mama yelled, Kelly could not have heard her. *This is not acceptable.*

I turn my body to face the door, but my head and eyes stay glued to Mama. As I walked slowly, I stared her down with intense eyes, the kind that could get your ass beat. I did it intentionally.

"What are you looking at, little girl? You better get your behind out of here before I spank you." She threw a pillow in my direction, but I did not flinch.

"Didn't I tell you to..." She got off the bed and came after me.

I ran into the living. When I looked behind me, there she was with her shoe in her right hand. I darted out the front entrance.

"Don't you bring your ass back into this house until I tell you."

When I reached the corner, I stopped running and leaned against a tree to rest. I thought for sure I would be running much further. I always seemed to press Mama's buttons. I guess I would play outside for a while. I watched two girls my age ride their bikes past me.

"I wish I had a bike." I kicked the dirt and watched it fly onto the sidewalk.

"Ouch." Slap! "Ouch." Slap! "Ouch." Slap. Something was biting me. I looked down. "Ants!" I swat them with my hands, but it pissed them off more. I was standing on their home, so they attacked my body – thousands of them. I took my tennis shoes and socks off, and sprinted on the neighbor's lawn so that I could put my feet in their sprinkler. I rubbed my feet forward and backward on the wet grass to make sure the water got them all. I tried not to get my shorts and t-shirt soggy. I glanced toward the front porch and the sign on the wall read, *The Kelsos*. They did not have curtains up to the window and I could see a large woman setting the dining room table. She had a nice smile. Two teenage boys and a man sat around the table, talking and having dinner – a typical scene in my middle class neighborhood. They appeared happy.

"I cannot wait to get older."

The onions and garlic smell from their kitchen made my stomach growl. I headed toward the house holding my belongings. When I got there, I threw them on the porch. I reached behind a potted plant for my plastic container, opened it, removed the sidewalk chalk from its bin, and drew hopscotch shapes. I found a rock near the shrubs.

"Look, Karen. That black girl is playing by herself with her crusty feet." She pointed at me. "Poor thing." Karen commented. They laughed.

I continued to roll the stone on the squares and tried to drown out their chatter. I believed they lived next door, but I was not sure. They appeared too old to care about having a conversation about me.

A car horn blared.

"Let's go, girls." The Bobbsey Twins leaped into a Chevy with a middle age man. He sped off trying to avoid the parked cars and the traffic coming from the opposite direction. Though it was a two-way street, it was too narrow for both vehicles to pass each other.

"I'm thirsty. I'll see if Kelly will give me some water." I approached the door and bellowed through the screen.

"Kelly. Kelly." I knocked.

"What?"

"Can you bring me some water?"

"No."

I banged on the door.

"Dana, stop pounding on my door," Mama retorted.

89

I sat down on the top step to rest for a few minutes. I heard thunder, but it was sunny. I shrugged my shoulders and then I pulled out my jump rope from underneath the glider seat.

"Cinderella, dressed in yellow…" I stopped because the cement hurt my feet when I bounced on it. I put on my gear and start again. I skipped with it up and down the sidewalk. I noticed a blue car driving slowly past the house. The man inside made me nervous. I remembered Mama telling Kelly not to talk to strangers and he looked pretty strange to me. Also, I kept my eyes on him. I made sure to remain in front of the house.

"Little girl, little girl, come here," he said.

I stared at him.

"Come on. I won't hurt you." I moved backward and stood on the bottom step. I could see his hands trembling. He jumped out the car with his lips purse.

"Mama! Mama!" I pulled on the handle to the door sideways. I did not want to turn my back on that lunatic, so I did not budge.

"No one will miss you. See, they won't even open the door for you." He gazed to the right to see if anyone noticed him, and then he turned to the left to do the same.

"Mama!"

He moved forward, then stopped.

"You are the ugliest thing I have ever seen."

He took another step, then halted.

"Mama, Mama!" I rattled the screen. "Please!"

"No one will miss a chocolate kid like you, not your family, not the community, not the media. No one!"

He grabbed my shoulders to pick me up. I twisted and turned several times.

"Mama! Help me!" I sang in a soprano tone.

I peered at the door and stretched my arms out, hoping to catch a hold of it. The angry man peeped in the same direction. That was when he let me go and scuttled toward his car.

"I saw you. I saw you before I came on the porch!" He pointed and laughed.

"Mama," I said with relief. She had been watching the entire event unfold and she did not say or do anything.

Damn her! Her calm spirit walked away. My stomach did the wheelies one final time – I guess the nerves resumed normalcy. However, I still could not open the door. I did not want to leave the porch, so I retrieve my jacks and tiny red ball from my pocket. I had no idea how to play, but I watched Kelly use them once. I actually stole them from her. I asked Mama for some, but she refused. Kelly could care less about them. Boredom set in after the fourth game. I bounced the ball up and down until I decided what to do next. It only took me fifteen seconds before I came up something exciting.

I climbed the oak trees in front of the house and sat on its branches that formed a seat. I watched some kids down the street play basketball without a net and two different neighbors watering their lawns. *I wonder why no one came to my rescue earlier.* I pretended to live on top of a mountain as royalty, looking down at the villagers who all lived in two-story brick homes with porches. I kept myself company by holding a conversation and answering myself. Every time I did it, Kelly would tell Mama that I had gone crazy. I did not care, I was not bothering anybody.

"Queen Dana, are you hungry?" I disguise my voice like a man. "Yes, sir, yes I am." "Okay, we will bring you a tray of food. What would you like? Bring me everything." I began to laugh.

I stayed up on my high branch until the streetlights came on, then I headed back into the house. My Mama waited by the door for me. She told me to sit on the porch until she was ready to see me. She served dinner to me on the porch consisting of baked chicken leg, corn-on-the-cob, and Kool-Aid. I ate and swapped mosquitoes in between bites. Mama cooked well. I had hoped to learn some lessons from her some day. However, when I tried to watch, she rushed me out the kitchen. I was not allowed back in until it was time for me to serve her plate. I always contemplated spitting in her food, but I was afraid she would catch me. I knew that day would be my last day on earth and I was not ready to die.

"All gone!" I commented.

"Mama, I'm finished eating. It was good!" I howled, knowing that she could not hear me.

Slap! "Gotcha this time!" I picked up the insect and stared at it. It wiggled twice, and then stopped. I threw it in the yard.

"What are you doing, weirdo?" Kelly asked, holding the door open.

I turned around and stared at her head, hoping she would think something was wrong with her hair and rush to fix it.

"Mama said come inside, wash your dishes, take a bath, and go to bed."

"Mama said come inside, wash your dishes, take a bath, and go to bed." I widen my eyes, trying to imitate her.

"Quit staring at me, darkie."

"Quit staring at me, darkie. Why don't you go fix your double head?"

Kelly huffed and left the doorway as it slammed shut. I tried to open the door but it would not open. I knocked on it.

"Kelly, you locked me out." I banged on the door. "Kelly! Kelly!" I banged more.

It got a little windy and dust blew on the porch.

"Kelly, please."

I banged so long that my knuckles hurt. I slid
down the screen and fell on the porch with one arm still
holding the door handle.

"K-e-l-l-y!"

I shook both legs up and down, and then I
whined. I felt raindrops on them. It started pouring
down on a slant, wetting up the house and me. I jumped
up and knock some more. My shirt stuck to my body
and I picked at it in between knocks that escalated into
kicking the door. Two minutes lapsed and I was tired
again. I tried opening the door, and it opened without
hesitation. I stumbled through it, went back out to pick
up the plate and cup, and headed to the kitchen. I
walked lightly because I did not want to disturb Mama.
I was already treading on thin ice.

Chapter 7

"What are you staring at?" I asked my sister as she hovered over my bed with piercing eyes as if I had done something wrong in my sleep.

"You."

I turned over so that I did not have to look at her face.

"Oh, Lord! Where did this blood come from? What is this!" I yelled while looking at her hands. Kelly ran from the room. "Someone, help me. I've been shot! I've been shot!" I sat up in the bed and pat the puddle around me, and then my pajama bottoms. I did not want to move again just in case more blood oozed out. I searched for the wound. It appeared that it came from my abdomen. I lifted up my shirt, but I did not see anything. I touched my legs and they seemed okay.

"What the hell…what the hell is this?"

I pulled down my pants. My underwear was soaked in blood. I moved my right leg over the bed first. I slowly brought the left leg next to it. I did not take my eyes off my middle. I slid my body forward, touching the floor softly with my feet. Then, I ran to the bathroom to pee. I pulled my garments down to my knees and sat on the stool.

"Ahh! That feels good," I told myself.

I let the undergarments and pajamas fall to my ankles, and then I kicked them to the side. I turned up my nose in disgust. When I finished relieving myself, I stood up and looked inside the toilet. I saw a mixture of yellow liquid with red fluid. I flushed the toilet so that I would not have to look at it. I examined my pubic area and then noticed more watery goo streaming down my leg. I tried to wipe it before it landed on the floor, but I was too slow. I turned on the shower so that it could warm up.

"I cannot wait to wash this yucky stuff off of me."

€€€

"Mama. What am I supposed to do?" I asked politely.

"You're supposed to wear tampons or pads."

"Do we have any?"

"No, I will pick up some on my way home tonight."

97

"What am I supposed to do meanwhile? I cannot go to school like this."

"Sixth graders go to school like this all the time. You had better get used to it. You will have to deal with this for at least fifty more years. You are a woman now!" I heard a little sarcasm in her voice. She kissed me on my cheek – a rare occurrence.

"Ma, do you think Kelly has some…some…pads or something?"

"I don't know, ask her."

I went upstairs to Kelly's room to talk to her, but she had already left for school. I figured she got a ride. I searched her bathroom cupboards to no avail. I return to the kitchen to tell Mama.

"Mama. Mama!"

"What is it, Dana? I have to get going or I am going to be late."

"I checked Kelly's room and I didn't find anything to use."

"What do you want me to do about it? I told you that I will bring you something home after work."

"Can I at least stay home today?"

"No!"

"But, Ma!"

"But ma nothing." She grabbed her bag and headed to the door.

"What am I supposed to use?"

"Use a washcloth, paper towels. I don't care, just leave me alone."

I stood there listening to the clock tick and inhaling fresh coffee. My eyes became full with water, but nothing fell. I was amazed at what just happened. I did not know why I was surprised. My life had been that way from day one. I was just grateful that Mama's spells had gaps in them.

When Carl made a pledge to remain on his best behavior, it lasted for thirty days – the honeymoon period for everyone in the household. Then, he resorted to his old habits, including Angel. Mama found out when he packed up his bag, left her a note on the refrigerator, and never contacted her again. Afterwards, she went into a functioning depression. She did the basic things to get through the day and to take care of us. I became a little more independent as each day passed because she did not concern herself with me. I did not mind because I felt the same way about her. I played in my room by myself for the most part. When Kelly wanted to aggravate me, she crossed my threshold for a few minutes in her clown costume, then leave in her "bad seed" dress – running. I did not take smack from her. My strength grew as I did, and it continued to get powerful.

I got over my pathetic life moment. I thought about ditching school, but my Mama would kill me. Moreover, I loved school. I treated it as my haven for six hours a day.

I marched to my bathroom and looked in the linen closet for a old washcloth, hoping Mama would not notice that it was missing. I pulled down my panties and removed the wad of toilet tissue from between my legs. The commercials lied about its absorbency. I folded the cloth over once the long way. It seemed rather wide, so I folded it again. It should soak it up, I hoped.

I start walking around the bathroom, pretending I was having a normal day. I felt as though a shovel had been shoved up my ass. I lost my confidence real quick.

"There is no way women walk around like this."

I put on my tight jeans. I wished to God that it will hold everything in place until I got home. At the very minimum, it felt secure. I looked at my buttocks in the mirror. I glance for any signs of a big dooky coming from my booty. I did not see anything, so I walked wide leg until I got use to moving with my make-shift feminine pad.

€€€

After homeroom, I managed my new life as a lady. No one seemed to notice or paid attention to me, as usual. I had one friend, Clancy. I saw him in my last two classes. We met last year during lunchtime; we both sat at the reject table. We became instant friends. Our parents thought we were boyfriend and girlfriend since we talked to each other every day and hung out on the weekends. Little did they know, Clancy liked boys. He tried to keep it under wraps, but he heard the whispers.

When I saw him later, I would ask him if he noticed anything different. I loved his honesty. Matter of fact, I could ask him about this whole period thing. He had four older sisters.

€€€

"Hey, girl, what's up with your pants?" Clancy ask.

"What?"

"You have something on the back of your pants."

I felt horrified. I turned my back toward my locker.

"I started my period," I whispered.

"Congratulations!" Clancy jumped up and down, clapping.

"Stop it! Stop, you are making a scene." I gripped his shoulders so that he could halt all that bouncing.

"But, this is good news."

"No, it is not! I feel cranky, fat, and sluggish. In addition, I have no pads and now my pants are ruin. What am I suppose to do?"

"Here, take my sweater and wrap it around your waist. Give it back to me later."

I took the powder blue sweater, wrapped the arms in front of me, then tied them into a knot. *That Clancy sure knows how to dress.*

"What if I get something on it?"

"Girl, I'll just buy a new one."

"Okay, what about the sanitary napkin?"

"Let me think…go to the nurse's office. She should have some."

"Clancy, you are a genius."

"Thank you. Thank you very much."

"Okay, no Elvis impersonation today." I put my hand in his face and waved it side to side.

"I'll see you in fifth period…ahhh, no pun intended."

I rolled my eyes and slammed the locker.

€€€

"Now, when did you start your period?" the nurse asked me.

"This morning."

"Is this your first period?"

"Yes."

"Did you tell your mama?"

"Yes."

"Why didn't you bring your pads with you?"

"I forgot."

"Next time, stuff a bunch in your purse."

"I don't carry a purse."

"Oh, you will now. Ask your mama to give you one of hers."

I grimaced. "I will." I knew that I would have to get a purse from somewhere else.

"Okay, here are four pads. That should hold you until you get home."

I stuffed them in my book bag.

"Don't forget to wash and return the sweatpants tomorrow."

"I won't. Thank you." I really wanted to say bless you, but since the school had gotten strict about religious, God, and such, I left it at that.

As soon as I walked into class, Clancy winked at me. I handed the teacher the note from the nurse's office and sat down next to my friend. That was the first time since I left the house that day that I felt at ease. The next class seemed as though it dragged on forever, probably because it was the last class for the day. When the bell rang, I rushed to my locker. I just wanted to go home, lie down, and watch television. Clancy trailed behind.

"Hey, girl, I have band practice so I will see you later. Call you tonight."

"Okay, and thanks!"

Clancy wagged his hand in the air without turning around.

€€€

"What's wrong with you?" Kelly asked me as I lay in bed with the pillow between my legs in a fetal position.

"You know what's wrong. Why are you playing dumb?"

Kelly came inside my room and sat on my bed. "Periods are the worst, I know. It gets better the older you get."

"I hope so."

Kelly rubbed my back slightly. "It will."

"Kelly?"

"Yes." She turned around before exiting.

"Is it true that I can get pregnant now?"

She hesitated before responding. "Yes."

"I've read some stuff on the Internet about this period thing and all. I had no idea that this can go on for seven days and… "

"Are you and Clancy planning on..."

"No!"

"Whew, that's good."

"Have you?"

"No, silly."

Slam!

"That's the door, it must be Mama," Kelly said.

We both ran down the stairs to greet her. I was more interested in getting a fresh change in my drawers. She gave both of us bear hugs. I could not believe it. I usually got the pat-rock-pat-pat hug. Work must have gone well. She went into her office and I followed her, hoping she would pull out the goods while Kelly returned to her room. Mama placed her satchel on the desk, took out some papers, and tossed them on the file cabinet.

"Did you bring them?" I asked.

"Did I bring what?"

My face tinkled and heated up.

"Did you bring the pads?"

"Oh, no. I forgot."

"You forgot?"

"Yes, I forgot. You better watch those lips."

"What am I suppose to do about the leaking in my pants?" I stormed off before I could say something else. I went to the kitchen to phone Clancy, but Kelly was using it. *Her cell phone must be charging. I cannot wait to get me one.* She had a conversation with her girlfriend for two hours and Mama stayed in her office. That was everyone's routine most nights. No one really cooked dinner or ate together. I made a snack when I got home, mainly pizza rolls and a root beer. Then, four hours later, I ate another one. I would narrow my choices down to hot dogs, cereal or a frozen dinner. I tried experimenting with fried chicken once, but Mama forbade me from messing around in her kitchen, especially anything fried. She claimed the grease smell makes her nauseated. Kelly's fame in the kitchen was grilled cheese sandwiches, macaroni and cheese, and frozen cheese pizza. She would eat one of those most nights. Mama would have a cup of coffee or fruit. She snacked on healthy foods all day to maintain her girlish figure. I suspected that she ate before coming home. On her late nights, she probably dined with a new beau at some fancy restaurant. She had been playing it loose since Carl left her.

"Hi, Clancy." He answered the phone on the third ring.

"Hey, Dana. What's up?"

"Nothing much. Guess what?"

"What?"

"No pads."

"What!" he shrieked. "Damn, your mama is cruel."

"I know."

"Can you hold on until the morning?"

"I think so. I will probably have to wear this same one all night."

"Okay, I'll see what I can do."

"Thanks!"

"You know I gotchu."

I hung up the phone. I darted back and forth for no reason other than to pass Mama's office and roll my eyes at the cracked door. I could hear her pecking away on the computer.

€€€

The next morning, I met Clancy at his locker. He handed me a decorated bag with handles that had a plastic bag peeping over the edges. I looked down into it and saw it was an economy size package of Always. I opened my mouth wide, but nothing came out. Clancy kissed me on the cheek.

"You are welcome. Now, get to class."

I smiled and headed to the bathroom first. Luckily, the washcloth that I used this morning worked well. I was finally getting this period thing down to a science.

€€€

"You are coming to my house for dinner." Clancy seized my hands and pulled me in his direction.

"Okay. Okay, but let me call Mama first. You know how she is."

"Alright. Here, use my cell phone. Hurry. I'll be over here."

Clancy pointed to a tree where three other boys were standing. I had never seen them at school before and they looked old. The redheaded one smoked a cigarette and handed it to Clancy. He did not accept it, and then he glanced at me and motioned for me to talk on the phone. I dialed my number, but no one answered. I left a message, letting Mama know where I was and when to expect me home. When I finished, I walked toward the gang. They scattered before I reached the area.

"They got out of dodge fast," I said to Clancy.

"Yeah right." He pressed down on my shoulders with his hands.

"What's your mother cooking tonight?"

"I don't know. Whatever it is, you will enjoy it." I pressed my lips together instead of saying anything.

€€€

"The lasagna was delicious, Ms. Prejean, thank you." I shared my gratitude with Clancy's mom.

"You are welcome. Now, go play. I'll take care of the dishes."

"I'll help you." I picked up my plate and glass.

She smacked my hands. "No, dear, that's my job. Now, run along."

I was speechless. Clancy yanked on me again. I shuffled along, still amazed. *This is how normal people do things? I do not understand why Clancy thinks his family is dysfunctional.*

"Move it, toots, before my sisters come home."

We walked into a Pepto Bismol pink room and straight into the same color bathroom. Clancy opened the linen closet door and dug his hand into the back. He maneuvered around the towels.

Slap! Crack!

"Ouch!" Clancy hit an A-note that could scare a cat.

I jumped. "What's wrong?"

"My hand. My hand. Help me, Dana."

"Let me see. Let me see." I pulled on his right arm.

"I cannot move it."

"What's going on in here?" Clancy's mother inquired.

Clancy drew his hand out and a mousetrap had him in a vice grip. His mother entered with towels in her hand. She dropped them and removed the contraption from his blue fingers.

"What ya'll doing in my room?" Brittney, the second oldest, wanted to know.

"You know," he replied.

"Your manicured hands got caught in our closet."

"Yeah!" the other three sisters chimed.

"I was just trying to get some pads for Dana."

"What?" I chocked on my own saliva.

"Dana's mama won't buy her any, so I've been stealing them from you." He pointed at each one. "You, you, you, and you."

"Is this true, Dana?" Ms. Prejean questioned.

I blushed and put my head down. "Yes."

"What!" The Prejean girls whispered. "That doesn't make any sense."

I was able to hear them.

Clancy's mother put her hand up to quiet her daughters' chatter.

"Well, when I go to the grocery warehouse, I will pick up the five hundred count instead of the two fifty. All four of them have periods at the same time. It is not a big deal to buy for one more person."

I did not know what to say, other than, "Thank you." I was so embarrassed, I barely said that. I did manage to tell them that Mama wanted me home early. Mrs. Prejean insisted that I stay for her dessert, homemade biscotti with French vanilla ice cream. I left right after.

"Where have you been?" Mama questioned.

"I was at Clancy's house. I called and left a message.

"What message, Dana? There is nothing on the voice mail."

"Are you sure? I called when I got out of class."

"How?"

"Clancy let me use his phone."

"Umm hmm." Kelly puts in her two cents.

I bet she deleted the message so that I would get in trouble.

"You know I don't like that boy."

"I know, Mama."

"I will check the answering machine." I walked to the phone to check.

"Don't bother."

"But, Mama, I swear that…"

"No more, Dana. Go to your room. I will decide your punishment later."

I walked out the kitchen, but I did not head to my room. I lingered in the living room and could hear Mama and Kelly talking about me. They loved ganging up on me, which was not very mature for a grown ass woman that I called Mama. *I guess looking young as me excuses her behavior.*

"Did you erase the message, Kelly, like I told you?"

"Yes, Mama."

My jaw dropped and I squinted my eyes. *Those dirty dogs. I knew that I left a message.* I went upstairs to use the phone. *Clancy is going to love this story.*

€€€

"Kelly, do you have any feminine pads?" I asked with sincerity. I needed some until I got my packet from Clancy's mom. She acted as if I was begging for a million dollars with all her sighs. She went to her bathroom and pretended to look. She opened and closed cabinet doors and drawers fast as if I was stupid. I was hip to her little games. She returned.

"No, nothing."

"Okay, thank you. If Mama buys you some this week, can a sistah get a few?"

"Why sure, anything for my sistah." She chuckled.

Once I left, she slammed her door behind me. I stopped to look back, feeling mad as hell. I headed to my room so that I did not have to interact with anyone. I sat by the door listening to my iPod. I watched Kelly's door to see if she left out. An hour later, she emerged. I peeped in the hall to make sure she was going downstairs. When I heard her hit the bottom, the door slammed. "She must be going out, good."

I tiptoed to her room and watched the stairs with caution. "I bet she lied about not having any." I started in her bathroom, and opened all the drawers and looked in the back. I tried not to touch or move anything or move it, I was afraid Kelly may notice. Then, I scoured through the linen closet. "Nothing." I looked under the cabinets and glanced behind the tub cleaner and near the tissue. "She is good." Next, I browsed her walk-in closet. There was so much stuff in here. "What's this?" I reached for a duffle bag on the top shelf. "Shoot." Her sweaters tumbled down on top of my head. "Damn." I rearranged them as best I could. I perused the bag, but I did not find the goods. I was so nervous; I could not stay in there to finish my snooping expedition. I scooted out the room and back to mine.

€€€

Every month for two years, Clancy brought me pads. Mama never once purchased them for me, but she did for Kelly on a regular basis. Mama told her not to let me use them because she bought them for her. The interesting part was that Mama never wondered or questioned how I got them. Once, I overheard Mama convey to Kelly, "…if I find out that you gave Dana some maxi pads, I am going to discipline you. And, you don't want to be on my shit list while in high school." Kelly hid them in different locations just in case I decided to trample through her things. I only did it when I was low or out, but sometimes I wanted to participate in a scavenger hunt. After awhile, it was not worth it. Kelly would notice something out of place and tell Mama. Of course, I get grounded for being in her room. She never got in trouble for going through my stuff. I still did not understand why Mama did not obtain them for me, other than she hated my skin.

€€€

"Well, kiddo, we are going to high school in sixty days," Clancy reminded me as the porch swing moved back and forth.

"I know. I know."

"It will be alright, Dana." He bumped my shoulder with his. I almost fell forward from my head's gravity, and then I concurred by nodding.

"It will not be that bad since you will be there." I rocked him back a little harder. His laugh turned into a frown and he put his head down. I swung my face underneath his. "Clance." He did not respond. "Clance?" I shook him to get him to speak. He stopped the swing before he answered. He turned to me.

"Dana."

I swallowed.

"I am moving to Edgewater, Florida.

"What? Why? When?"

"My dad got a promotion. Plus, he is on his final stretch before retirement and he wants to be in Florida."

"This means…"

"I know." He embraced me and then let go.

"You can always come visit."

"Yeah."

We did not say a word for at least two minutes. We listened to the sounds of the birds, the swing squeaking, and an ice cream truck down the street.

"When do you leave?"

"Two weeks."

"Two!" I stood up.

"Hi, Dana, you coming to the going away party?" asked Mrs. Prejean.

I studied Clancy's expression. He would not look at me. "Oh'um…yes, ma'am."

"Oh, I must have interrupted. I'll leave the lemonade here." She sat the tray down on the end table.

"When's the party?" I asked in a perturbed voice.

"Next weekend."

My eyes widened and my stomach fluttered for several seconds. A single tear plunged down my right cheek.

Clancy held my hand. "I promise to call, email, and Facebook you."

I could not help but giggle, if for no reason other than not to cry. I picked up a glass and Clancy followed suit. We raised them for a toast.

"To friendship," cheered Clancy.

"To friendship."

We tapped our drinks and sat back down to enjoy the rest of our afternoon.

It was the saddest day of my life – the Prejean's Party. It seemed as though everyone that cared for me ended up leaving. I would miss Clancy so much. I covered my face with both hands because I did not want to see myself upset, let alone my reflection in the bathroom mirror. I did not like the image that I saw.

There was a knock at the door. "Dana, you okay in there?"

It is Mrs. Prejean. I turned around before answering. "Oh…yes, ma'am. I will be out in a minute."

"Okay. I was just checking."

I pulled myself together and returned to the event. I was the last guest there. The immediate family members were in the kitchen. Clancy's two oldest sisters were staying in Nautica to complete college, so their spirits ran higher than the rest.

"Dana, come over here, please?" Mrs. Prejean stated.

"Alright."

"We all chipped in and bought a parting gift specifically for you."

What, for me?

"Oh no, Mrs. Prejean, the party favors by the doorway are fine."

She escorted me to a chair around the dinette set.

"Sit." She pointed downward and I obeyed.

Clancy delivered the decorative gift bag with handles.

"Shall I open it now or wait until I get home?"

"Now!" everyone ordered.

I nervously said, "Okay."

I placed the yellow tissue paper on the table. I stood in order to remove a box with sixty-four maxi pads. We all cackled until I started crying. Clancy wept, too. His mama hugged me and exited with the others. I suspected that she sobbed as well. Clancy and I held each other in the middle of the room. I could not phantom life without him. He brought color to my black and white images, hope to my heart, and oxygen to my leaves.

He released me, then he wiped my chin with his index finger. "That should hold you until you start babysitting," he managed to say.

"I agree." I sniffled. "I'll have to save my money to buy lots more." I sniffled again. "Ha! Ha! Ha!" I responded nervously to my own comment, not knowing what the future held.

Chapter 8

"Where are you going, Dana?"

"I am babysitting tonight."

"Okay, but make sure you return by midnight."

"I will."

I left the house in a good mood for a change and walked across the street to the Miller's residence. I was babysitting their two children, six-year-old Wyiatt and five-year-old Emma Jo. It did not take much to care for them. Mrs. Miller paid me twenty-five dollars per hour on the weekend and fifteen dollars for weekday, not bad money for part-time work. I would make sure to purchase my hygiene items and hide them. I was afraid that Kelly, or even Mama, would take and destroy them so that I could not enjoy them. They hated on me every chance they got. I had to look out for myself because no one else would. Clancy did, but he was no longer in my life.

I remember when I met the Millers. One day on my walk home, I saw a little girl on her bike with training wheels. She had fallen off and sitting on the sidewalk with tears streaming down her face. Though I did not know her personally, I had seen her plenty of times around the neighborhood. Her large brown eyes matched her curly brown hair her perfectly. Her parents always waved "hello" to our family, but no one took the initiative to introduce themselves.

"Hello. Are you okay?"

Whimpering, she said, "No, I want my mommy."

"Okay, can you walk?"

"Mm...Hmmm."

I picked up the overturned bike and turned it upright.

"If you get up, I will walk you home. Okay?"

"Okay." She stood up and I dusted off her knees. We walked side-by-side going toward her house. We made sure to not step on the weed-less sidewalk cracks or we would break our mother's backs – a game that I taught her during our short journey. Five feet away, she grabbed my hand. By then, she had stopped crying.

"Emma Jo! Emma Jo! There you are!" a woman who could be her mother shouted hysterically. She picked her up, and hugged and kissed her.

"She's fine. I found her down the street. She had fallen off her bike."

Mrs. Miller was a petite woman with blond hair and double D boobs. She looked like a size double zero. The diamond ring she wore probably weighed more than she did and it blinded me as I talked to her. She studied me for a moment.

"Thank…"

"Dana," I interrupted. "I live across the street." I extended my hand.

"Oh…that's where I've seen you. I appreciate it."

"I told her not to go far. I thought her brother was with her," she tried to explain as if I was the police.

"No problem, anytime. We have to look out for each other, right…" I placed my hand on the girl's shoulder.

"Emma Jo." Her mother shared her daughter's name.

She nodded and put her head on her mother's shoulder.

"Oh, and this is Wyiatt."

I leaned down so that I was eye to eye with him. "Hello, Wyiatt."

"Hi," he responded, holding on to his mom's pant leg.

"Dana, have you ever done any babysitting before? You are good with my kids."

"No."

"Would you like to?"

"Well…okay."

"Alright. My husband and I are going out on Saturday around seven. Is that good?"

"Yes, but let me double check with my Mama first."

"Okay, just let me know." She began rattling off her number and I committed it to memory.

"I will. Thank you."

€€€

I arrived home at ten o'clock, two hours before my appointed time. Life was good. I worked three hours and had seventy-five dollars in my pocket. I opened the front door with ease, hoping not to disturb anyone. I sashayed into the kitchen to get a glass of water. A sliver of light beamed from Mama's bedroom door. She sometimes read before bed. I slipped my head in to see if she was awake, as well as to let her know that I was in the house. In my mind, I thought she worried about me and she waited up to ensure my safety. Usually when I talked to her, it confirmed that I was way off on my thoughts.

I could hear the clock fizzing, the big hand always tried to make it past the twelve on the hour. I laughed and walked toward Mama's room. I tapped lightly, however, I did not hear a response. I moved the door.

"Mama, you sleeping?"

She turned over on her side to face the wall. I took that as a yes. I would check in with Kelly as a backup. I could let her know that I was home. After all, she would look at the clock to see if I was late. She loved witnessing me getting in trouble. If I was overdue one minute, she would make up a lie. I was her source of entertainment since she had no life, at least not according to my standards. Some would say the same about me.

I double-checked the back and front doors, turned off the lights, and trotted upstairs. When I reached the top, I could her soft music playing behind Kelly's door. It sounded like Alicia Keys.

126

"Kelly, you awake? Kelly?"

"Yes. What is it?"

"I'm in."

"So what."

I raised my brows and continued to my room. I had no idea what she was doing, but I could guess even if she was alone.

I wanted to shut my door in order to hide my money, but Mama disliked it when we did. She would say, "There are no secrets in a house where I pay the bills. What goes on behind closed doors should be seen in the light." Kelly did not obey the rule. I did because I had consequences. I figured since everyone was preoccupied, I should be fine not shutting it.

I walked into the closet, opened up the sock drawer, pulled out a taupe knee-hi stocking, stuffed the money down in it, and tied a knot in it. Then, I stuffed it inside one of my old shoes – a Sketcher. That was my version of a Wells Fargo safe. A chill in the air gave me goose bumps, so I turned around to look at the door. I could have sworn I saw a shadow. I proceeded to the doorway; nothing looked disturbed or unusual. It could have been my imagination, paranoia or nerves. I prepared for bed by turning down the comforter, drawing my bath, and finding some nightclothes. I soaked in the tub for thirty minutes. The lavender water relaxed me the same way it did when I was a baby. Before I turned off the light, I wrote a list of things that I wanted to do with my dough. Most went to savings, hair products, and "personals." I said a silent prayer and drifted off to sleep.

€€€

I sat up in the bed and sniffed. *Why I am smelling bacon?* I looked at the clock and saw it was seven thirty a.m. I washed my face and brushed my teeth. I passed Kelly's room, but I did not see her. I entered the kitchen with caution. Mama and Kelly chatted over partially eaten food.

"Dana, come join us."

Kelly's comment sounded fake. I looked at them strangely, just in case I was sleepwalking. I glanced into the pan. I saw eggs and bacon sitting there. I put two pieces of bread in the toaster and sat down.

"What's the occasion?" I asked.

"Mama won money playing the lottery scratch off game," Kelly reported with enthusiasm.

"Really?"

"Yes. She decided to treat us with breakfast."

"How much did you win?"

"Not enough to take us to a nice restaurant, but enough to buy a few items for a meal."

"That's cool."

Plop!

"Good, my toast is ready."

I spread butter and raspberry jam on them and took a seat again, but that time I placed myself at the counter. I was still groggy, so I did not say anything.

"How was Emma Jo and Wyiatt?" Mama asked.

"Oh…good, they weren't any trouble."

"Um…hmm," Mama responded.

Kelly giggled. I looked at her and so did Mama. They acted like weirdoes from the *Twilight Zone*. Lottery winnings or not, something did not seem right. I cleaned my plate with the last bit of bread. I fetched the orange juice out of the refrigerator and guzzled down a full glass. I ran back upstairs so that I could get out of the zone. It made me nervous, which did not sit well on a full stomach. They finished eating, but continued talking as if I did not exist.

I put on my clothes and cleaned up my bedroom. I wanted to go shopping and did not want Mama to say anything about my chores. I made the bed, vacuumed, and dusted the furniture. The bathroom would have to wait until the next day. I hated cleaning that room; I put off doing it all the time. Mama usually had to threaten me before I took it seriously. *When I get older, I am going to have a maid.*

"What are you doing?" Kelly inquired.

"Baking cookies for my tea party."

She rolled her eyes and disappeared.

"What are you doing? What's wrong with her, asking stupid questions? Mama needs to have her evaluated!" I laughed.

After five minutes, Kelly came back to my room.

"Mama said that we are going to the mall. Be downstairs in ten minutes."

"What?"

"You heard me, slave girl."

Mama really must be in a good mood. The mall? I did not even have to ask, scary. I rushed to the closet to get my loot. I dug in the shoe and withdrew the stocking. I unknotted it and jerked out a wad of newspaper.

"What the hell. Where is my…"

"Are you ready?"

I charged Kelly, knocking her down.

"Stop, get off me, you bitch!"

I tried to claw her eyes out, but I kept missing. I tagged her face instead.

"Mama! Mama!" she screamed.

Mama ran toward us and pulled me off Kelly. "Stop it! What is going on here?"

I kept swinging at the air.

"Stop it, Dana!" Mama held me back.

I kicked the air.

"I said stop it, dammit!"

I breathed erratically, but my nerves were calming down.

"What is going on?'

"Kelly stole my babysitting money."

"I did not. That girl is crazy."

"Dana, are you sure?"

"Yes, I am sure."

Mama turned her head. "Kelly?

"I don't want anything that tar baby has."

"There you have it, Dana, she doesn't have it."

I moved my arm with force so that she would release me. *One of you bitches have my money and I want it back.* I stared at Kelly, hoping to break her demeanor. I could not get a response. *Maybe she did not take it, which means only one thing, Mama did.*

"Dana. Dana, go to your room and calm down."

"I am calm!" I yelled.

"Well, go clean your bathroom. I'll talk to Kelly."

"I did."

"Well, go do something. Move it now!" She pointed.

I knew something was going on around here. They both were in cahoots, stealing money from a kid. I could not prove it nor could I think of any other explanation. They were two mean females.

I withdrew the cleaning products from underneath the cabinet and slammed the door shut. I scrubbed the sink with some elbow grease.

"Talk to her? She is not going to talk to her, more like laugh at me and go shopping to buy themselves something. Mama did not cook nor shop with her kids. Those heifers took my money and now they were going to throw it in my face." *Who needs enemies when you have family?*

I finished the bathroom and layed on the bed to collect my thoughts. I was upset with myself for destroying Kelly's face. I reacted without thinking. I guess all my animosity broke out a can of whoop ass. I probably would have killed her if Mama was not there to save her.

Mama came in the room and dropped on the bed. I did not have the heart to even look at her. She reached into her wallet, pulled out money, and threw it on the bed.

"There. There's your damn money."

I reached for it slowly as if it were going to bite me. I picked it up and counted it. "Seventy five dollars? What's this for?"

"It's your money."

My eyes widened. "Where did you get this?"

"Let's not play games. You know where." She stood up. "I decided to return it."

"Return it? Why did you take in the first place?"

"I told you about keeping secrets and hiding shit in my house. I wanted to teach you a lesson. I never anticipated you trying to kill your sister over money, you black, ungrateful witch."

I looked down in shame, but only for fighting with Kelly, not for hiding my own money. I waited for the punishment.

"No more babysitting for two weeks."

"What? No!"

Kelly appeared in the doorway.

"I am sorry, Kelly."

She stared at me and positioned herself to appear as a back up for Mama. They reminded me of some gangster chicks.

"Kelly doesn't want your pitiful apology. She wants revenge. I told her I would have none of that in my house."

I glanced up to see if I was listening to the woman that I called Mama.

"Instead, I am removing your bedroom door from its hinges."

"What?"

Kelly handed her the tools with a Kool-Aid smile. They begin removing the hardware one by one. I was stunned and saddened. I did not use the damn thing, anyway, it was the fact that I lived in hell everyday without a clear leader. I tended to excuse Mama for her immaturity because she had me at a young age. However, she defied the odds and became a successful person in comparison to some of her peers. She insisted on being uncivil to me because I was dark skinned. *Well, I cannot change my hue, but I can change my heart. I refuse to be hateful, inconsiderate, and rude to others. I got carried away this time. Lord, forgive me*.

€€€

After my two-week sentence, I spent the summer getting ready for high school, babysitting, and reading. I stayed out of Mama's way and she stayed out of mine. She did not hang around the house since she found a summer fling to keep her preoccupied. She did not talk much about him nor did she bring him to the house. Sometimes, I heard her and Kelly snickering. I guess they swapped man stories. I really did not care, I was just happy that she left me alone. It was all good for Kelly, too, because it elevated her from being Mama's pawn in the hate relationship against me.

"What are you doing?" Kelly asked, munching on chips and guacamole.

"I am going through the Sunday paper looking for back to school sales. See my list of supplies." I held up the notepad and resumed flipping the pages.

"Wow, how much money does babysitting pay these days?"

I glanced at her and continued browsing. I wrote paper, pens, and index cards down, and folded the ad close. I did not worry too much about clothes since I wore uniforms to school. Mama bought me no-name jeans and basic shirts with no style to them. I got Kelly's designer hand-me-downs. I did not mind because I was not into fashion.

I gathered my things and headed to the Thrift Store. It was several blocks over, but I did not mind the walk. The neighborhood had not changed much since I was a child. The brick homes and the neighbors were older. Some days, the streets were deserted and there was not a child playing outside within miles.

136

When I arrived, I searched the missy shirt section for white button-down shirts.

"Here we go."

I inspected two short-sleeves and one long-sleeve blouse. They looked dingy, but nothing bleach could not cure. When I got home, I put them in the wash. After I took them out the dryer, I ironed them to put creases down the arm area and hung them in my closet.

I searched the Internet to price the school's plaid pants, shorts, and skirts so that I could share the information with Mama. I was hoping she would contribute. My bargaining strategy was to tell her that I planned to purchase my own accessories, shoes, and socks. If she hesitated or refused, I would throw in my own undergarments. *Decent bras and panties are expensive.* I have already selected a new pair of glasses from the Seeing Is Believing Vision Store. I can pick them up a week before school starts.

I had a regular babysitting schedule for summer, 8 a.m. to 1 p.m., Monday through Thursday. I was off on Friday, Saturday, and Sunday unless Mrs. Miller needed me for a special occasion. I did not have to

137

worry about cooking since she prepared the meals ahead of time and posted the daily menu on the icebox door. I just heated the food in the microwave or served them cold, depending on the item.

"Today, guys, we are going to the park and the library."

"Hurray! I love the library," Emma Jo rejoiced.

"Well, I like the park," Wyiatt added, disclosing his preference.

"Okay, I am going to pack our lunches in the picnic basket."

The modern ones were the best. They had a section for hot and cold items. It sat on wheels and operated similar to a Pullman bag. I adjusted the handle upward to test it.

"How cool is this?"

"Way cool." Wyiatt chuckled at me.

"Let's head out." I waved them toward the door.

We strolled one block in the blazing sun, and I felt as though I needed a gallon of water. Good thing we did not have to go further. The kids ran to their favorite area while I found a shaded picnic table. Lucky for me, I caught a breeze every now and then. I sat there reading the last few chapters of my vampire book because I had to return it to the library. Anything with those bloodsuckers was a winner in my eyes. However, I read my Bible before I go to bed – how ironic. I guess I pray for peace while I sleep.

I let the children play for one hour before reeling them in for lunch and a drink. If I did not, they would continue until they had a heat stroke. After chomping down on crackers, cheese, and sliced summer sausage, they devoured ant logs, celery smeared with peanut butter and topped with raisins, for dessert. They were the only kids that I knew that did not drink sodas; they consumed water with their meals. Afterwards, the Miller's were ready to go. I did not mind, I needed an air conditioner break. We loaded up our things and headed back toward the house. The library was two blocks in the opposite direction. It would allow me to put away the leftovers and the family could use the restroom.

We got to the library in time for the storyteller, so the dynamic duo squat in the front of the room while I relaxed in the back with the *Architectural Digest Magazine*. I had been exploring the architecture field on my library visits. Shapes and drafting fascinated me. I usually studied magazines and books for hours until it was time to leave. Of course, I would grab a good fantasy book on the way out the door.

Once I finished browsing the magazine, I planned to practice what I learned. I had a free *Home Builders Magazine* that I swiped at the grocery store. They had pictures of homes with accompany floor plans. I tore out the perfect ones and put them in a scrapbook. I made my own modifications to the others that needed some adjustments.

I whipped out the pencils and ruler, and went to town. I flipped through several pages, folding the edges of those I would rip out later. "Here…" I stopped on page ten. "Let's add a half bathroom near the kitchen." *Did that lady just give me the "mama look" or am I imaging things? For a moment, I thought it was her. I guess I was speaking rather loudly.* I put my head down in shame and shifted my eyes side to side, hoping no one else heard me. I did not see how the animated narrator thought the room was her stage and we were the props without getting into trouble. I rose up in my chair to get a better visual of the youngsters; they were having a good time. I sat back down and resumed my project.

I had a vision for my dream home, husband and kids. I knew what kind of mother and wife I would become. I observed and learned from others what to do and what not to do. Unfortunately, Mama fell on a side all her own – obtuse. "Ha!" I covered my mouth in time so that I did not disturb anyone. I made sure I remained silent throughout my stay.

€€€

"What are we doing today, Miss Dana?" Wyiatt inquired.

"A movie and the pool."

"Hurray!"

I was glad that we walked to most events. However, we took the bus to the movies. Emma Jo and Wyiatt found it a special to ride. I agreed, but for different reasons. During the summer, theatres offered free movies for children. They started at ten in the morning on Mondays and Wednesdays. I treated them to one menu item as long as they promised to behave, and they did for the most part.

My work and hobbies kept me sane. I could not think of a better place to be in my mind – a summer break from Mama.

Chapter 9

"Who is your sister?" Some random student asked me who was surrounded by two girls that looked like her. They were not triples, but they had similar features. Dressing in the same outfits did not help.

"Kelly."

"Are you sure?"

"What?"

"Are you sure Kelly Calhoun is your sister?" She laughed and her spectators joined her.

I did not answer and I could hear them laughing as I walked away with my head held high. *Bitches.*

I might not have looked the best, but I was boney, five feet eight in height with high cheekbones – model material. The greatest part was that I knew that I was smarter than most of kids at that school. They hated it and intelligence was not cool to them. Making fun of my chocolate skin was an easy target. They did not have anything else to criticize other than comparing me to Kelly. However, her looks were all she had going for her. She made below average grades and Mama did not even say anything. Her philosophy was that Kelly's beauty would carry her far. I tried to explain it to them like Judge Judy, "beauty fades, dumb is forever." They could care less. When I leave high school, I plan to go to college and I will become successful. I was in honors classes and on the college track schedule. I found the honor students to be more accepting of me, probably because everyone else thought we were nerds. I did not mind, my own Mama had called me worse.

I was friends with my biology lab partner, Sheila. She wanted to become a biologist in her adult life and she took all her classes very seriously. I enrolled in all of them except for last period. She had an independent study course with the chemistry teacher to earn college credits while I was stuck in first year Spanish. She knew that she would be in school a very long time. I, on the other hand, planned to go to a four year college in another state and get a degree in Architecture. I had no plans on going beyond that for a higher degree.

"Class, put your pencils down and pass your papers forward," Ms. Abernathy told the math class. She surprised us with a quiz.

"How did you do?" Sheila asked.

"I think I did okay."

"Cool. I'll see you in the lunchroom." Sheila rushed out.

I walked to the cafeteria, hauling most of my books in my backpack. I was so afraid that I would be late for class if I ran back to my locker. When I arrived, the line winded out the door. I stood there; mad at myself for not bringing a lunch. The mixture of burnt cheese and applesauce made me dry heave.

"Hey, sis!" I turned around to see Kelly staring at me and smelling like fruity gummy bears.

"Hey, you know you cannot cut."

"I am not trying to cut. I need to borrow some money for lunch."

"What?"

"I need some money for lunch." She did random sign language with her hands as if I did not hear her.

"Your precious mama did not give you money, or she did not have time to make you a lunch today?"

"Look, are you going to give me the money or not?"

"Not!"

"Oooo…" the girls behind me chime.

I looked at them with a smirk on my face. It read, "Mind your own business."

Kelly shook her head side to side. "You ugly bitch. That's why our mama hates you!"

The entire line heard the outburst, laughed, and started pointing at me. Some even repeat what Kelly said. I ran outside to the courtyard to get some air. It already had a crowd and the chatter sounded like the Wall Street Stock Exchange, but I managed to tune it all out. I threw my book bag down underneath a tree, pulled out a textbook, and sat on top of it.

"Here you go," a strange male voice said.

I looked up, but the sun blinded me and I could not see his face clearly. His arm extended in front of my face and he handed me an apple.

"Here."

I was so hungry that I took it. It did not matter that I did not really know him.

"Thank you."

"No problem."

He walked away before I could say anything else. I bit into the apple, grateful that someone cared.

"There you are," Sheila remarked and parked herself next to me. "I bought you a sandwich from the al-a-carte line."

"Thank you."

"Someone told me what happened. Why is your sister so mean to you?"

"I don't know."

"I am glad that I am the only child."

"You are lucky."

"Yeah," she responded.

"Yeah," I concurred.

We sat there talking about our classes and homework until the bell rang. We hopped up and headed to our next class. On the way, I saw the boy who gave me the apple. He looked at me and headed in the opposite direction. I had never seen him before that day and did not know if he was a freshmen or upperclassman. I thought about him the entire period. I wished to see him before the end of the day.

€€€

"Made it!" I shouted as I crossed the threshold of the classroom door. I walked to an available seat in the front and plopped down.

"Today, class, we are having a brief presentation by freshman, Roger Goodwin, on the new Green Project at Montgomery High School. He will be here shortly. Meanwhile, clear your desk for a ten minute pop quiz."

"Aw," the class moaned.

"Great. Just great," I whispered to myself. Even though I studied the night before, I still do not like surprises, let alone a quiz.

The classroom door opened. It was the guy from lunch.

"This is Roger Goodwin, folks. I guess we will have to wait on the quiz."

"Yeah!" the crowd cheered.

"Please, give him your undivided attention. Thanks."

"Hello, class, my name is Roger Goodwin..."

I did not hear anything after his monotone introduction. I watched his full lips quiver with each word. I moved down to his thin torso. His shirt read, *The Green Machine*. It looked too tight because I could see his stomach impression. *I wonder if he has a six-pack.* Then, I stared at the bugle in his jeans. When he moved side-to-side, it budged with him. He shuffled so much that I got mesmerized with his thing dancing. If he talked much longer, I would start to hear music.

"… and that's why it is important that we recycle. I will bring a paper only recycle bin for your classroom. The cans and plastic bottles bins will be housed on the first floor near the cafeteria. The newspaper receptacle will be in the teacher's parking lot. Thank you for your time. Any questions?"

"Anyone have questions for Mr. Goodwin?" the teacher asked.

Do you have a girlfriend? I thought about asking, but I saved myself from the embarrassment.

No one did and he rushed out the room. I did not even know if he noticed me. Since I knew who he was, I could search for him on MySpace.

€€€

"There he is, Sheila." I pointed at the computer screen.

"Let me see." She walked over to the desk and looked over my shoulder.

149

"Very nice. Very nice," she commented on Roger's profile picture. "You gonna talk to him tomorrow?"

"What would I say?"

"I don't know. Say something to him."

"What if I don't see him?"

"You will. You harassed the poor student assistant to give you his class schedule."

"I did not harass her. Plus, I have to give her five dollars tomorrow."

"Anyway… He is cute, nice and environmentally conscious. What more do you need?"

She put her hands on both of my shoulders. "What do you have to lose?"

I rolled my eyes at Sheila and hit the button on the computer to send a friend request. Then, I stood straight up, marched to the bed, and fell forward onto it, stiff as a board. I did not move because I was contemplating my next move with Roger.

€€€

I looked for Roger all day to no avail. *Where can he be?* I figured that if I ate lunch again in the courtyard, he would reappear. I brought my peanut butter and jelly sandwich, hoping that was the case. I went outside and looked around, but I did not see him. Sheila promised to join me if he was not around. I sat there for a moment before diving into my peanut butter and jelly sandwich. Out of frustration, I took a huge bite.

"Hey there!" I heard a familiar voice behind me.

I looked around the tree. *It is Roger. Damn! My mouth is full and peanut butter is stuck to the roof of my mouth. Hurry up and sallow.* I coughed.

"You okay? I did not mean to scare you."

I nodded yes, but I still could not speak. I raised my index finger, anticipating he would give me a second before walking away.

"Hi, Roger. How are you?" I coughed again.

"I am good. Thanks for the friend request on MySpace. I accepted it this morning."

"Cool."

The awkward silence made me wonder if his shyness would prevent him from asking me out on a date. I did not want to seem desperate, but I was. I never had a male who showed any kind of interest in me. If they did, it was to get next to Kelly, the pretty one. I guess smarts did not mean much to guys, however, Roger seemed different. He did not fall in the popular group, but he did not belong at the other end. He dangled in the middle, which meant the invisible man – seen when necessary or beneficial. I did not make the radar at all. I thought people tolerated me because of my sister.

€€€

"Hi, Mama. This is Roger."

"Hi, Roger."

"He came over to study with me."

"What for?"

"What do you mean?"

She inspected him up and down, then me. "What I mean is; why he chose you to study with out of all the girls at Montgomery?"

I did not say anything. I just look at her with droopy dog eyes.

"If your looks do not kill him, your body odor will."

I inhaled. Then, I grab Roger's arm and dragged him outside. I choked before speaking.

"I cannot do this."

152

"Do what?"

"Study with you. She is so cruel." I gazed toward the door.

"I am not worried about that. I have to pass my classes, graduate, and go to college. If I concern myself or divert my plans every time someone says something, I will never amount to anything.

"You right, you right." I touched his lower arm.

"I know I am right.

"Do I really smell?"

He hugged my right arm. "No, it's her imagination. Come on, we have work to do. Plus, I would tell you if you were a little tart."

I laughed so hard that I got lightheaded. I composed myself and walked back into the house. We hurry up the stairs because I did not want to give Mama a chance to say anything smart.

"Leave the door open!" she yelled.

I paused on the step wanting to say something, but I did not. Roger hit my back with his nose. He snorted, then I continued walking. I passed Kelly's room and glanced in to see what she was doing. She and Darryl, her boyfriend, cuddled on the bed and she sat on his lap. She slammed her door before I made it to my room. I switched my hips like a princess as I walked across my doorsill.

"Nice place," Roger commented. "I like the color." He viewed the wall behind my headboard.

"Thank you. I painted it myself as an accent. It's a periwinkle."

He walked over to my dream home collection of architectural drawings hanging on the wall. I chose my top three to display. My favorite hung in the dark purple picture frame. Though I found all three of them about two years ago, I figured I could narrow my choices with the help of my future husband. I hoped that he would like them. If he did not like at least one, I could always update it to suit his likes and dislikes. I thought about marriage and family more often since I discovered the opposite sex. Designing dream homes only heightened my desire. I figured that I would find someone in college in spite of Mama's belief that I would end up a forty year old virgin with twelve cats. I did not even like the feline hairballs. I would graduate, find a job, get married, build my dream home, and have children – all in that order.

Roger gawked at each one as if trying to decide on his favorite. When he finished, he did not say anything and I did not ask.

He sat on the floor, not wanting to disturb my bedding or give the appearance that he sat on it. I think my Mama made him nervous. I pulled out the antique white chair from underneath the desk and faced him. I removed my workbook from my backpack. Our first order of business was to take the practice exam for the Preliminary Scholastic Aptitude Test (PSAT) and score each other's. I planned to take the test next year and wanted to get an early start. I figured that if I did a little each day, I would be awesome when I actually took it. Roger agreed and jumped on the bandwagon.

Umm…Umm..

Squeak. Squeak. Squeak.

Aw. Aw.

"What's that noise?" Roger asked.

"What noise?"

"Listen."

I stopped turning pages so that I could hear. I tilted my head to the right so that I could concentrate.

"Umm…Daryl. Daryl…yes…baby...yes."

Squeak. Squeak. Squeak.

I dropped my jaw in disbelief. I glued my eyes to the Dance Theatre of Harlem poster on the wall as if I had x-ray vision and was able to send a signal that said, "Shut the hell up." It did not work because the sound increased.

"Do that shit."

Slurp. Slurp.

Squeak. Squeak. Squeak.

I put my hand to my mouth to resemble someone throwing up. Roger's eyes widened.

The noise made him uncomfortable, so he covered his package with his book as if I did not notice. After all, he sat on the floor Indian style. He tried to resume normalcy, but it did not work. His fair skin could not hide his blushing cheeks. I, on the other hand, was disgusted. The thought of my big sister having sex in the room next to mine repulsed me. I banged on the wall to let them know that I could hear them. Hopefully, Mama did not hear me because she would cuss me out for hitting her walls like that. I was sure Mama heard them because they were so loud – no shame in their game. The sound stopped.

I heard Kelly laughing. *What is so funny?* I shook my head side to side and continued working on a math problem.

"Stop! Stop! Stop tickling me!" Kelly shrieked.

"I really wish she would be quiet," I said to myself.

"Me too," Roger concurred.

I did not think he could take it much longer. I avoided looking in his direction, thinking that may relax him. I had ten more questions to answer before our discussion, so I buried my head in the book. It remained quiet for thirty minutes, then Roger and I were ready to talk about our answers. I could not tell if his wood declined, he did not move or adjust his position the entire time. I figured his legs would get tired eventually. I scored ninety-six percent and Roger received one hundred on the math portion. His intelligence excited me and he had better grades than I did. However, that did not matter to me because I could learn a lot from him. One day, I would be number one.

"Well, I better get going," Roger commented. He tried to stand up and cover himself with his books. He grabbed his book bag with his right hand and held on to his book with the left. He swapped them out so fast I did not see anything. I did, however, squint my eyes. Good thing he did not notice. He jammed the book inside and the bag dangled in front of him.

Wow, I thought that it would have gone down by now. I am impressed. I escorted him to the hallway. I stood at the top of the stairs waiting on Roger to hug me, but he did not. I guess "woody" still embarrassed him. He ran down the stairs and out the front door, making sure not to slam the screen. He did not even look to see if Mama was around.

Before I made it back into my room, Kelly's friend exited her room. When he shut the door behind him, a foul odor gushed out the room. I turned my nose up and stared at him. He did not acknowledge me. He shuddered down the stairs and out the door. A minute later, Kelly emerged in front of my door.

"You hungry?" she asked me.

"Yes."

"It's snack time!" we sang in unison, so we trotted downstairs to make grilled cheese sandwiches. Mama poured coffee grounds into the coffeemaker.

She resembled a zombie and I figured she must have just woken up.

"I heard you and Roger upstairs having sex," Mama commented.

"That was not me, it was Kelly."

"Is this true, Kelly?"

"No, Ma, I would never have sex in your house."

"See, Kelly follows the rules of this house."

"It wasn't me!"

"Since you cannot, Roger is no longer welcome here."

"It wasn't me, it was Kelly! This isn't fair!" I slammed the block of cheese down on the counter.

"You have a problem with what I said?"

"No, but it…"

"I don't want to hear anymore about it. Now, go to bed, the both of you."

"What?" Kelly questioned.

"Bed, now, go." She pointed toward the ceiling.

Kelly and I exited the kitchen at the same time. I bumped her shoulder with mine on purpose.

"You make me sick," I mumbled.

"You are just jealous, you ugly virgin," she responded.

"What?" Mama inquired.

"Nothing!" I answered, giving Kelly a cold stare as I proceeded upstairs.

€€€

The next day, I sat in Smoking Joe's Coffee Lounge waiting on Roger. "I hope he gets here soon." I glanced at the clock hanging over the exit sign and fidgeted with my books. I ordered a mocha latte with a shot of espresso and it had me jumpy. In addition, I had to get home by five o'clock. I wanted to spend as much time with him as possible, even though we would be studying. I pulled out my calculator and notebook to appear as though his delay did not bother me. The glass door swung open fast. *It is him*!

"Hey, Dana!"

"Hey." I stood to hug him and ended up in his armpit, inhaling his lumberjack deodorant. I did not mind.

"Sorry I am late."

"No problem." I played it cool.

"I'll make it up to you. Whatcha having?"

160

I touched my empty Styrofoam cup and shook it. "Oh, this, I'm fine." *And, so are you.*

"Okay, well, I'm going to grab something, then I'll be ready."

I waved. He smiled, showing off his two dimples. I watched him interact with the barista. *He has so much charisma.* One of the characteristics that I required in a man. I placed my elbow on the table, cupped my chin with my hand, and tilted my head. I drift into daydream central.

"Dana?" He snapped his fingers.

I saw fingers and nothing else.

"Dana?"

"Sorry." Roger broke my trance.

"I am back. Let's get started."

"Roger, first I have some bad news."

"What?"

"You cannot return to my house. Mama thinks you and I were doing the nasty yesterday."

"What!" He alarmed the other patrons. They could not help but to peer in our direction. I put on a nervous grin.

"What!" he responded in a softer tone.

"I tried to explain, but Kelly lied."

He positioned his hand to indicate stop. "I don't want to hear anymore. I would n-e-v-e-r… no problem. Let us just call Smoking Joe's our spot for our freshmen year."

"Sounds good." *I guess. What did he mean by never?*

€€€

Once a week, Roger and I meet at Smoking Joe's to study. On the weekends, we went to the movies or the mall with a group of mutual friends. We tried to hit all the festivals so that we could partake in the amateur thrill rides. Mama threw salt in our game plans by having me do tons of chores. I got around it by doing them all fast or by telling her that I had to babysit. She did not mind since it relieved her of some of her parental responsibilities such as buying me toothpaste, soap, and shampoo. I used Sheila as my other scapegoat, though Mama did not care much for the girl. She said, "Sheila acts too bougie and she does not ever make eye contact with me." I thought Sheila's smarts intimidated her. Mama found it in her kind heart to let me slide, however, when her man friend visited

162

from out of town. That charade continued for the entire school year.

Once I started my sophomore year, Mama got tired of cock blocking and she allowed Roger to return to the house. However, we had to study in the kitchen and she had to watch us. I did not care because Roger was back in the house. Let me hear the people say, "Whoot! Whoot!"

Chapter 10

"Hi, Roger," Mama spoke when she entered the kitchen.

"A, hi, ma'am."

"You here again?" she asked.

"Yes, ma'am. We are studying. Trying to get ready for standardized exam, they are tomorrow."

"Oh yeah, I remember those. It determines if you pass to the next level, right?"

"Exactly."

Mama nodded her head. She never acknowledged that I was in the room, but it did not matter because I was used to it. I continued punching numbers on the calculator. Mama poured herself some coffee and left the room. Roger leaned over the table and kissed me on the forehead. I took it as a sign of compassion in house with none. He stopped trying to understand it. His parents were very respectful and affectionate. They functioned like a real family, at least on the surface. That was why I loved him so much. He knew what to say and do at the right time.

"One more problem and I better get going."

"Okay." I looked at him.

As soon as he started talking, I began to reminisce about our first kiss. I graduated to intimate kissing during the summer, none of that friend stuff anymore. *June seemed unseasonably hotter than usual. I had finished babysitting the Miller kids and their cousin. Roger picked me up via foot patrol at the cousin's house. On the way home, he took me to the Ice Cream Social, an overpriced ice parlor, to cool down. He ordered a root beer float with two straws. The vanilla ice cream floated above the rim, so we both jabbed it with our straws, then dove in full force. We leaned forward with our forehead almost touching, our cheeks sunken in, and lips pursed, trying to penetrate the ice cream so that we could reach the liquid. We wiggled in our chairs to get a better handle on the situation. It became so intense, our heads touched. I stared into his brown eyes and he gazed into mine. He moved his creamy lips toward mine. I closed my eyes and went for it. I felt the earth move. When I opened my eyes, it was the chair moving from underneath my behind.*

"Woo! Oh!"

Bam! Boom! Crash! The chair tumbled onto it side.

"Dana, you alright?" Roger asked, helping me off the floor.

"Yes. I'm okay," I lied. My bum hurt like hell. I tried playing it off when the cashier came running over to assist me.

"…and that's how I arrived at my answer. Got it, Dana?"

"What?"

"Got it? Did you hear what I said?"

Lying, I said, "Yes."

"Okay, so tomorrow we will meet in the cafeteria for breakfast and go over some last minutes testing strategies."

"Perfect." I jiggled my head in agreement.

He gathered his books and stuffed them into his book bag. I walked him to the front door and he turned around to get a kiss. I tilted my head back and stood on my tiptoes to reach his lips. He leaned over slightly. I pushed so hard that he fell backwards into the door.

"Oh sorry, I don't know my own strength."

He laughed. "I know. Good night." He hurried out the door.

I shook my head and I watched him down the street. *Poor guy.* When I turned around, I jumped. Mama stood in the foyer glaring at me. I gave her a half smile and trotted back into the kitchen for my things. It was going to be a long night of studying.

€€€

I sat at my desk reading passages and answering questions so that I could improve my comprehension. Then, I practiced doing word problems, my weakness. I had no clue why I needed to know where two trains leaving at the same time from two different cities met. I managed to get the right answers every time, but it took me forever to figure it out. Some would not consider that a limitation, but I did. I needed to learn how to compute faster and accurate – a trait I considered important for a future architect.

€€€

My cell beeped and I looked at it. Roger let me know that he made it home and settled.

...happy studying and have a good night. I read the rest of the text aloud. I smiled and continued with my work with a little more energy.

€€€

Bump!

"Ouch! That cell phone hurt. Aw, man." I rubbed my forehead with my right hand, then my right eyes, trying to get mucus out the crevasse. *I cannot believe that I fell asleep and hit my head on the cell phone. Good thing no one was here to witness that, I would be so embarrassed.*

"I cannot go to bed yet, I have more to do. I will go get some coffee."

Once near the kitchen, I notice Mama's office door cracked and the light illuminating. I walked down to see what she was doing.

"Mama?"

"Yes?"

"Why are you still up?"

"Working. Why are you still up?" she asked me.

"Working."

"You need to go to bed."

"I will, Ma. I am almost finished."

"Okay, but don't wake up bitchy in the morning."

"I won't, but if I am not up by five thirty a.m., can you get me up a half hour early? I want to meet Roger for breakfast."

"Alright, I will. Now, go to bed and no coffee."

"Ma!"

"No coffee or you will be up the entire night. Go to bed, Dana." She sounded agitated.

"Going." I inhaled a whiff of coffee as I passed the kitchen, hoping it would jolt my body. The burnt grounds almost made me gag. I had done all-nighters before; I did not know what the big deal was that time.

As I climbed the stairs, I could not help but think about the freedom that I planned to have when I moved out the house. When I get to the top step, my eyes felt heavy. I could hear Kelly snoring behind her closed door, a snort that ended with a purr. I did the zombie walk to my room, sat at my desk, and turned off the cell phone. The screen looked blurry, so I missed the off button twice before getting it right. I could not take it anymore. I needed to take a short nap, then I would be refreshed again. I lay in the bed. *I just need five minutes.* Before I could adjust my pillow, I descended into a deep sleep.

€€€

I sit straight up in bed. "I'm up! I'm up!" I yelled to the echo of what I believed was mama's voice ringing in my ears. "What time is it?" I reached for the cell and turned it on. The message indicator light flashed with three voice mails. I moved my clock around so that I could read it clearly. "Ten twenty one? This cannot be right. What the… Ma!" *I must have forgotten to set my alarm when I came back upstairs from talking to Mama. "Shoot!"* I flipped the covers back.

I flew into the hallway and did not see any commotion from Kelly's room. I traveled downstairs to find mama, but did not locate her in her bedroom or office. *I will check the kitchen.* When I entered, I gazed at the clock on the microwave. It read, ten twenty three. "What? What? Oh, Lord. Oh, my goodness. I am so late."

I could hear my heart beating in my ears. I hoped I do not have a heart attack. Why did not mama wake me? Damn her! Damn her!

I run upstairs to the bathroom to brush my teeth. Then, I comb my frizzy hair backward and put it in a ponytail. I changed my shirt, slipped on my shoes, and darted downstairs.

The front door opened. "Dana, you are finally up? I did not think you would ever get up," Mama told me.

I felt as though I was dreaming. I waited a second and blinked hard before answering her, thinking that she would disappear. She did not. "What are you talking about? You know I have to go to school. Why didn't you wake me?"

"You just looked so peaceful sleeping this morning, I just couldn't do it."

"Ma, you know I have that test today. I told you to wake me up early so that I can meet Roger for breakfast." My voice moved up an octave.

She acted like a Stepford Wife, moving and speaking methodically. "I know, but I figure you should get your rest." She walked into the kitchen with the grocery bag. I followed her as if time had no value or importance to me.

"Ma, you realize that you may have jeopardized my high school graduation?"

"You are over reacting, Dana. Go to school."

"You did this on purpose. You don't want me to graduate." I grabbed her hands so that she would stop unloading the bag.

"Have you lost your mind? Let go of me." Mama pulled her hands backwards. Then, she gripped my throat with both hands and pushed me up against the refrigerator. My head hit it with force and I started getting lightheaded. I was a foot shorter than her, so she looked down and pressed her nose up against mine. I smelled bacon grease on her and figured she must have gone out to her favorite restaurant for breakfast. She stared into my eyes.

"Don't you ever! E-v-e-r! Touch me again. Do you hear me?"

"I can't breathe?" I put my hands over hers, hoping to pull her off me, but I could not bring myself to do it.

"Do you hear me?"

I nodded. She released her right hand and slapped the left side of my face.

172

"Say yes, ma'am to me." She hit me again, but harder. My glasses moved to the right a bit.

"Yes." I coughed. "Ma'am."

"That's better."

She is going to kill me. Mama is going to kill me. Please, Lord…Our Father who art in Heaven…

She finally released me and I slumped down to the floor. I did not know what else to do.

"You ain't shit, just like your father. Look at you." She bent over my head, bumping her tennis shoe up against mine. She inhaled, then exhaled. "You stink. Why don't you bathe sometimes?"

I sat there lifeless like a Raggedy Ann doll. I watched tears drip to the floor. They started forming their own puddle. If I could drown in them, I would. Mama's voice got louder. I tried to block it out, but it became more irritating, as if she knew I was not paying attention.

"You skinny, pathetic bitch, you. Your nasty, black skin looks dry. Why don't you use lotion? Oh, I know why. Mama will not buy me anything. Woo! Woo! You don't deserve a damn thing. All you care about is you and that fifthly hair." She pretended to

173

touch it with the tip of her finger, but jumped back. "Ouch, your hair cut me. Comb that shit sometime, why don't ya."

I prayed silently to God that she would end her tirade so that I could go to school.

"You don't love me," Mama bellowed.

"Yes, I do! I do love you! I have always loved you, Mama."

"No you don't. You never have. You were put on this earth to make my life miserable. Well, Miss Darkie, you have succeeded."

"I did not ask to be born."

"I thought you would look like me or at least be a boy, but instead, you look like a female version of Sambo." She did a heal-toe jig.

I lifted my head. "May I go to school now?"

"Are you looking at me?

"Yes, I can see you."

"Can you see anything with those coke bottle glasses?"

"I see you clearly, Mama."

That time, she sang and pranced around the kitchen. "Can you see me? Can you see me?" I did not respond. I waited for her to answer my question.

"Get off the floor and take your stupid ass to school."

I rose, making sure to kept my head down and not make eye contact. I touched my throat, hoping she did not leave a noticeable mark. I sensed her staring at my back as I exited. I went to my bathroom to examine my face. *I am beautiful*. I thought. *I am beautiful. I am smart. I am...*

I dropped my eyelids. "Not today, you will not steal my joy. Not today." I squirted a dab of lotion in my hand and rubbed it around my eyes and mouth. "Not today." I closed the bathroom door.

€€€

I went into the office to see Ms. Murphy, the school's guidance counselor, so that I could get a pass to class. She seemed like a helpful and understanding woman, at least she came across that way when she assisted me with preparing my class schedule the past two years. She would say, "Dana, you know that you don't belong in regular English, you should be in honors level. The teacher is excellent and she challenges motivated students to shine. You need to shine."

"May I speak with Ms. Murphy?" I asked the student aide. She popped her gum before answering.

"Her office is in the back. If it's open, you can talk to her. If it isn't, you cannot." She pointed toward the office without turning around.

"Umm...thanks." I walk past the other worker, an upper classman, and the principal's secretary.

I knocked on the door. "Ms. Murphy, can I come in?"

"Sure, Dana. What can I do for you?"

I sat down in a wooden chair in front of her desk.

"Why aren't you in class?"

"I just got to school."

"You just arrived? Wait. What happened?"

"I overslept."

"Dana, this is a very important test day. You can't be late."

"Too late now. I need a pass to class and I need to make up what I missed."

"I don't think you can. Sorry."

"Please, Ms. Murphy. I need to…"

"Dana, it won't be fair to the other students. I cannot let you do that. The teachers will be upset with me. Oh, let us not forget the students as well as the parents and the entire faculty." She spun out of control with her example, making me feel helpless.

I did not have any more tears left in me to cry. All I have were fighting words.

"Ms. Murphy, I know for a fact that Friday is a test make-up day. Why can't I do it then?"

"Because those students have legitimate reasons for missing, like sickness, hospitalization, and funeral. You were simply irresponsible.

"Ms. Murphy, do I have a history of being irresponsible?"

"Well, no."

"Then, why you go there? While I am here talking to you, I am missing my very important test day. I have only missed three hours of the test. What is three hours on Friday going to do to me?"

Ms. Murphy blew out a breath. She wobbled from behind the desk to the door and shut it. She pulled a twin chair next to mine. I could see her worry and passion in her eyes.

"I will see what I can do, but no promises."

I put my right hand over my heart and close my eyes for a few seconds. "Thank you."

"No promises, Dana."

"I know." I jumped up with anticipation of going to class.

"Let me give you a pass."

Ms. Murphy grabbed the tablet off her desk and wrote me an excuse. She was probably someone's mother, may be even grandmother. I bet she never choked out her kid. I shook off the disturbing thought as she handed me the note.

"Thank you again." I grabbed the paper and ran out the room.

"Slow down, you are already late," she yelled down the hall.

I opened the door to homeroom. Everyone glimpsed up from their test and I handed the teacher the note.

"They have ten minutes left on this section. You can join them on the next one. Why don't you go sit in the back until they are ready," he whispered.

I walked past Sheila. She gave me the strange eye and mouthed the words, "What happened?"

I mouthed back, "Tell you later." I gave her a crooked smile. *I have a great lunchtime story for her.*

€€€

"Ms. Calhoun, may I see you for a moment?" Ms. Murphy asked me. I turned to Roger, held up my index finger, and walked over to her. "I'm glad that I caught you before you left school. I talked to the principal. You need to report to the cafeteria at seven am sharp on Friday for the make-up exam.

I gave her a quick hug, trying not to draw attention to us. I smiled as if I just won the Miss America contest. "Thank you. Thank you. Thank you." I waved goodbye and walked away. Roger and Sheila waited outside the front door talking. I could not wait to tell them the news.

€€€

I entered the house with caution. I did not know what to expect from Mama nor Kelly. I traveled to the

179

kitchen, threw my books on the table, and picked up an apple from the fruit bowl. Mama came in with Kelly.

"Hi, guys," I cheered.

"Oh, hey, Dana," Kelly responded.

"How was school?" Mama asked.

I looked at her. "You know what, Mama? It was great!" I smiled at them both. I snatched my books, pushed my shoulders back, and held my head high. I walked out the room. I heard them snickering, but I did not turn around to entertain them. I believed that I had conquered that battle; I had nothing else to say.

Chapter 11

"Do you see your mama and sister?" Sheila whispered to me.

"No." I looked around the audience for them. The top graduates sat on the stage facing the spectators, so I could see everyone pretty well. "I hope they make it before my name is called."

"They will."

"You don't know my family."

"You are right. They are kind of strange."

I bumped Sheila's shoulder with mine, and then laughed. Someone told us to be quiet. I chuckled again out of spite. I had become sassy as a senior and I did not care since I was leaving all my classmates behind. I did not have to interact with them ever again unless I chose to do so. Sheila would head to Massachusetts Institute of Technology (MIT), and I was going to Columbia University in New York. I would visit her and she planned to visit me. Roger decided on New York University. Someone tried to accuse us of cheating since we were the top three in our class and friends.

"Please, give a warm welcome to this year's valedictorian, Sheila Cotton. Sheila, it is time for you to address your graduating class," Principal Wu chimed.

"Thank you. Thank you so much. What an honor it is to stand before you…" Sheila began.

Unfortunately, I tuned out the rest of her speech. I listened to her recite it about forty times the night before, so I knew it backwards and forwards. I had to find Kelly and my Mama. I started in the far right corner and scanned the audience again, that time slowly. *No hands waving, nothing is sticking out that resembles them.* Kelly promised that she would make it. *Perhaps, her plane were delayed. I hoped not for my sake.* After she graduated three years earlier, she dumped her high school sweetheart and moved to Dallas with her girlfriends. She took several classes at the community college, then dropped out, claiming her Mav's Dancers schedule became too demanding. I think it was because she got caught dating her college professor for grades. Now, she dated a married Maverick's player on the down low.

There she is. I see her, she made it. I do not see Mama, though. Maybe she went to the ladies room. I kept my eye on that spot the entire time. I still do not see Mama. When the principal called my name, I stood at attention and marched ahead.

"Dana Rae Calhoun salutatorian, grade point average four-point…"

"Boo…boo…boo…" some students retorted.

"…full scholarship to Columbia University."

The crowd cheered wildly, drowning out the haters. The kids on the stage clapped with vigor. We hoped to reach our goal of getting more scholarship and grant money than the previous classes. I had enough to pay for my books, room and board, and tuition for four years.

I reached for my diploma and glanced in my family's direction, but I did not see anyone. I hugged the graduation committee and sat back down. The principal called Roger's name, he had a three point nine. He, too, received a full scholarship. He had to maintain a three point zero in his major, business. He planned to attend law school after he got his undergraduate degree.

When the ceremony ended, I encouraged my friends to participate in a group hug. At that moment,

Sheila's parents snapped a picture of us. I gave them a squeeze and shortly thereafter, Roger's parents walk up. I clinched them as well.

"Where are your folks, Dana?" Roger's mama asked me.

"They are somewhere in this mess." I pointed at the gang of people surrounding us.

Roger changed the subject by holding his mother's hand and slobbering all over her cheeks. She loved it. He was a mama's boy. Then, he grabbed his dad's hand and gave him a one-arm hug.

"Dana! Dana! Dana! *There is my sister.*

"Kelly!" I screamed. "You made it! You made it!" I held onto her as hard as I could and did not let go until she started crying. I missed her. Before she left home, we became friends. I guess maturity pumped through her veins and finally made it to her brain. The name-calling subsided and she stopped letting Mama manipulate her into hurting me. When she did, Mama left me alone and found a new hobby, photography. I guess when there was no audience, why perform.

Kelly checked on me from time to time by phone and email. She even sent me care packages –

nothing homemade, but fun eclectic items such as books, CDs, and fingernail polish. I even talked to her about boys and school. No matter the topic, she listened and supported me.

"I am so proud of you, Dana."

I pulled away, looked at her in those brown eyes, and embraced her again. Sheila started crying and Roger walked away to avoid looking at us. They knew how much seeing my sister meant to me. Roger's mama snapped more pictures.

"Where is Mama?"

Kelly shifted her eyes left and then right, and then she looked at me. "She wasn't feeling well."

"I see."

"But, I got some pictures. I ran down to the front to make sure I caught the moment on my camcorder. I'll show her when I take you home."

"Oh, okay."

"Let's get a group photo of the top three graduates," Roger's mom suggested.

I stood in the middle with my long legs and slanted my head to the right. Roger stood on the right of me, put his arms around my waist, and tilted his head to the left. Sheila positioned herself on the left with her arm around my waist and her left leg lifted in the air in front of us. I placed my left arm around her shoulder since she was shorter than I was.

"Say cheese!" Roger's mother told us.

"Cheese!"

€€€

I opened the door to Mama's bedroom. She slept silently. I went inside to give her a kiss, something I never did. I could hear her breathing. It sounded like a wheezing sound. I leaned over and kissed her on the forehead. She opened her eyes slowly and blinked them continuously as if to focus. She moaned and moved over on her side away from me. When I turned around to walk to the door, Kelly watched.

"Dana, wait." She reached for me, but I bumped into her and walked past.

I went to my room and Kelly followed behind me. I began taking off my graduation gown and clothes.

"She didn't even wake up to say congratulations, no hug, no smile, nothing. What did I do to deserve this? I asked myself this my entire life."

Kelly sat on the chaise lounge and listened.

186

"From the beginning, it's been nothing but hell, pure hell. But, I have been the good child by trying to love my family unconditionally."

"Dana, it is not that bad."

"Shut up! You shut up! You have always been the pretty one, the popular one, the favorite one. Look at you now. What have you done for yourself? I would not want to be you."

Kelly jumped up with her mouth open. "That's how you feel about me?"

I exhaled and shook my head side to side. "I am sorry. I did not mean it like that."

"I heard you loud and clear, but just for special effects, what did you mean actually?"

"You know what I meant. You have always had things handed to you. You have always been loved. Folks show it to you and not even know you. I…"

"I know what you mean. You don't have to keep going. Did you really mean that you don't want to be me?"

"I meant it because I am who I am. I am blessed with book smarts. You were born with looks."

"Why do you say this? You are beautiful girl."

"One, I am below average compared to you. Two… wait… since when have you had a change of heart?" I waited for Kelly's response, but the awkward silence filled the room.

"Yes, I've changed. I'm mature now."

We both laughed, breaking the tension in the room. Kelly and I returned to the lounge together. I put my hands on top of hers.

"I love you, Kelly. You all I have."

"I love you, too, Dana. You are all I have."

"What do you mean? What about Gabe?"

"He still around, but I don't have all of him. I share him. When he finds out I am pregnant, he will probably get rid of me."

"What?"

"I am pregnant. You are going to be an auntie."

"Me, an auntie?"

"Yes."

"When? How far along?"

"I am due in eight months."

"Have you told Ma?"

"Not yet. I will tomorrow."

"What do you think she will say?"

"I don't know, but I want you there when I tell her."

"I will be there. You know I got your back."

She smiled and embraced me again. I liked her much better as an adult than I did as a kid. I think the feeling was mutual.

€€€

"You are what?" Mama questioned in disbelief.

"I am pregnant," Kelly replied.

Mama continued pecking on the computer. She did not look at Kelly. I parked myself on the brown leather couch and Kelly occupied a chair in front of the desk. I felt as though I was getting ready for a business decision to go down. Finally, Mama stopped typing and stood up. She stared intently into Kelly's eyes.

"Congratulations!" She hugged her and her demeanor changed.

"Thank you, Mama."

"I am going to be a grandmother."

"Yes, in about eight months."

"Do you plan to get married?"

"Not now."

"Okay. Does the father plan to help you?"

"Yes, ma'am. He will make a great dad and he will take care of his responsibility."

"Great, because I cannot help you."

"I know, Mama. I did not ask for your help."

"Good." She sauntered out the room.

We both looked at each other with roving eyes. We decided to go find out where Mama went. We discovered her in the kitchen preparing dinner. Something was definitely up. Neither one of us wanted to say anything. We just watched her make spaghetti and meat sauce, salad and garlic bread. We set the table as a team and when the food finished, Mama put it all on the table. We gathered at the dinner table together and before we began, she said grace. My skin crawled with the anticipated news. I could not wait until she spilled the goods. I tried to get some indication by staring at her, but I could not imagine what she was about to say or do.

"Amen," I repeated. I felt awful missing the prayer. I was consumed with all my own thoughts. *Forgive me, Lord.*

"Mama, this is so good," Kelly told her, smacking her lips.

"I have cancer," she sprang on us.

"What?" I asked, putting my fork down.

"I have stomach cancer. I found out today. I have to start chemotherapy immediately."

My forehead and cheeks got a warm sensation and I started hyperventilating.

"Dana, you okay?"

"Yes. I am fine. I just need to get some water." I ran into the kitchen while Kelly consoled Mama.

My head hurt. I could not believe what I just heard. I felt bad for Mama and I knew that I could not do anything for her. Then, my heart filled with guilt about going away to college. I could not help but wonder if she fabricated the story and threw in a meal for good measure or theatrics. *Is this her way of getting Kelly and I to stay home? But why? She does not like me. I know she misses Kelly being at home, but this is a dirty trick.* I returned to the dining room.

Mama's chair faced outward while Kelly was crotched in front of her. They hugged and cried together at the table. I stood there watching as usual. I did not know what to say, I had always been on the outside of their party. I put my head down and placed my right hand on my forehead to gather my thoughts. I pulled my shoulders back and lifted my head up high. I swallowed.

"I'll just stay here and go to school."

Kelly and Mama turn to look at me. "What?"

"I'll just stay here and go to school." I took two steps toward them, walking as if I was dodging a land mine. "I can go to the tech college. They have an architectural design program. Plus, I can finish in two years."

"No. this is not an option for you," Mama told me.

I was confused and I hoped it showed on my face. I was trying to help her. Again, she rejected me, even in her time of need. *She is ready to get rid of me, out her hair and life for good. How cold can a mama be?*

"You are going to New York, end of discussion. Anyway, Kelly said that she will move home."

I stared at Kelly in disbelief and bobbed my head up and down. *I guess that is the best move for her. Is she just doing this to make me feel guilty?*

"Kelly, are you sure?" I asked.

192

"Yes. I am already struggling to pay bills. Plus, this will give Mama the opportunity to spend time with her grandbaby. Gabe will understand."

I took three more steps, the last one landing me in front of them. I kneeled and looked at them eye to eye.

"I am going to miss you guys." I put my arms around them and waited for Mama to react. She did not. She took the hug like a champion. I did not cry, but my heart wept for her.

Chapter 12

"Oh, my goodness, when will this end?" Kelly whined as she heaved in the toilet.

"Why are you asking me as if I know this stuff?" I responded, pulling a strand of Kelly's hair out of her face.

"You are the smart one."

"Oh yeah, I forgot."

"Hear I go again!"

"Okay, I got ya. Now lean."

"Wait, one more!"

"Oh man, I have this unbelievable pressure on my abdomen, like someone is making lemonade out of me."

"Honey, you are no lemon. My poor niece or nephew needs to stick with me. Lemon? Where do you get this stuff?"

"Shut up." Kelly kicked me on my leg.

"Hurry up. I need to go check on Mama."

"Alright, alright! I am almost empty."

€€€

I tiptoed down the hall so that I would not disturb Mama. I wanted to check on her since she had chemo. It made her weak and nauseated as well. I opened the door slowly as if the crick decided to take a break today. Crick. *Damn!*

"Who's there?" Mama asked. She turned over in her bed to get a better view.

"It's Dana. How are you feeling?" I approached her and rubbed her shoulder. She moved to the side and did not say anything.

"Do you need anything? I brought some creamy potato soup from work. I can heat it up." I started a part-time job at The Bread Box the day after graduating. They were great about hiring young people for the summer. I only got two days out the week. The other time I spent babysitting or chill'n with Roger – the two long-term things in my life.

She picked up the television remote and turned up the volume. I knew my queue. *She must not be in the mood today,* I thought sarcastically. "Fine. I will bring you some, anyway."

"Dana?"

"Yes."

195

"Shut the hell up and close my door behind you."

I put up the peace sign and left the room as ordered. I did not let her ruin my spirit because I had been having a good day thus far. I made twenty-five dollars in tips and I only worked four hours. It all went into the college fund so that I could buy bedding, school supplies and towels.

I entered the kitchen and start cooking. *Kelly might eat with me tonight.* I poured the soup into a stockpot and moved the stove knob on low. I pulled out the frying pan and threw some bacon in it. I leaned over the stove to get a whiff of the grease. It crackled and popped, but I was fearless.

"What are you doing?" Kelly asked.

"Oh…making dinner."

"You?"

"Um, yeah. Are you dining with me tonight or praising the porcelain goddess?"

"We will see."

"Dana, are you in my kitchen cooking?" Mama yelled from her room.

"No, it's Kelly!"

Kelly wagged her index finger at me. I shrugged my shoulder and kept on flipping the bacon. Then, I covered the pan with a lid. I pulled out the cutting board and green onions. I felt like a gourmet chef. Watching the Food Network finally paid off. Kelly watched in disbelief as I used the knife the appropriate way. *I had better learn how to do something for myself before I go to college.* Next, I pulled out the grater to shred some cheese. I moved the heat up a little more on the pot because my bacon was almost finished. I grabbed the sour cream from the fridge, the crackers out the cupboard and place them on the counter. *Perfect. Even though it is soup, I am going to serve it like a baked potato.*

"Well, Kelly?" I waved the aroma in her direction.

"I'm having what you are having." We laughed in harmony, so much so, it disturbed Mama. She appeared in the kitchen. We both looked at her in surprise, but we did not show any emotion. Her lifeless eyes seemed fake, like she had a corona transplant.

197

"Come join us," Kelly told her, getting a bowl out the cabinet, trying to seem as though she cooked. I knew Mama knew the real deal. She always knew.

Mama broke her trance and she found the energy to get orange juice out the icebox and pour herself a glass. She sat on the barstool, drinking it in slow motion while I prepared the dish. She appeared old, tired and worn down. I felt bad because I could not do anything for her, like cure her disease. I smiled at her as a sign of family bonding. She did not react. *I tried.* I let it bounce off my shoulders as always. *That's just Mama.*

I waited for the harsh criticism about her kitchen, but it never came. We ate together in silence and I took it as a sign that everyone was enjoying their food. I still had my guard up as Kelly and I cleaned the kitchen. Mama watched, making sure we did everything right, I assumed. She never said a word about me not rinsing the dishes before putting them in the dishwasher. *Man, she really must be sick.*

€€€

After dinner, we watched a movie in Mama's room. Kelly lied in the bed with Mama while I relaxed

198

in a chair next to the bed. She did not allow me to lounge that close to her. I propped my feet on the ottoman so that I could at least appear comfortable while in Mama's room. I never spent that much time in there. I tried to enjoy the moment since I longed for acceptance in Mama and Kelly's clique. When the film ended, Kelly and I arranged the furniture back like we found it and gathered our popcorn bowls and empty cups. Mama fell asleep before it went off and I pulled the covers over her chest. Then, I kiss my fingertips and swung my hands in her directions, hoping it would reach her in her dreams. I could not think of a better way to show my affection without getting flack for it. Kelly smiled at me as if I did a good deed. I put my head down and exited.

€€€

"Are you sure that you are going to be okay here with Mama?" I asked Kelly.

"Yes. Now go. You have been helping both of us. You need a break, you need Roger." She pushed my back with both hands as I walked toward the hallway.

"Okay, okay…I'll go get ready."

"Ah! No! Lord, no!"

"That's Mama," I told Kelly.

"What is that crashing noise?" she inquired. We ran downstairs, taking the steps by two. I grabbed the door handle, but it did not turn. We pounded on the door.

"Mama! Mama! Are you okay! Mama, open the door! Open the door!"

The door swung open and Mama stood there weeping. Her eyes were red and her hair a mess. I swallowed, hoping the oldest would take over. I did not know what to say to her without being ignored or worse, cussed out. When Mama leaned to the right, Kelly caught her just in time. I joined in to assist and held on to her left arm. We guided her to the bed and she fell down.

"Look at me," she said.

"What, Mama?" my curious mind begged.

"I don't mind losing a few pounds, but now my hair is coming out. Look at it. Look at it." She angled her head down so that we could see. We examined it for her and saw she had three patch spots.

200

"I can't keep doing this. I love my hair. I don't want to lose anymore."

I chose to remain quiet until I was invited to speak. I was taking a risk by sitting next to her. Kelly caressed Mama's tresses and listened. The rhythm of her strokes put me in a stupor. I started thinking about my own hair and the whole relaxer fiasco – yet another selfish thought on my part. I could not help wonder if it was payback for all the hurtful things that she did to me.

"I have an idea," Kelly interrupted Mama's tirade and my thoughts.

"What?" Mama responded.

"Let's go wig shopping."

Mama thought about it for a second, then agreed.

"That should be fun," I chimed. They both looked at me as if I was an alien from another planet.

"Yoo-hoo! It's me, Dana. I'm not gone yet." I waved as if they were far away.

"Well-a, okay," Kelly said and continued her up-down motion.

I turned my head toward the television as if it was not a big deal. Mama took a leave of absence from work when she first started treatments. She spent most her time at home with Kelly. When I tried to include myself in their reindeer games, I got the deer with the headlight looks. I waited a minute, then left the room. I could hear Kelly explaining to Mama what kind of hair would enhance her face.

€€€

"Hey, Roger. You want to hang tonight?" I asked the love of my life.

"Sure. I'll bring over Chinese and a movie."

"No. I need to get out this house."

"You can come by here; my parents are out of town."

"Umm…why don't you come here instead? We can have an Asian picnic." I had been avoiding his sexual advances so much, I wondered if he sought the goodies from somewhere else.

"Dana, we are heading out. Are you coming?"

Before I could answer, Kelly was halfway down the stairs. I ended my call and rush to the door. "Where is Mama?"

"She is in bed. She wants us to pickup something young and hip from the Beauty Barn."

"Okay, let's get moving. I have a date."

ϵϵϵ

"What about this one." I dangled a reddish brown wig in the air.

"No!" She held up one next to her face to get an idea for Mama's complexion. It took us an hour to purchase two wigs – a human hair one and the other synthetic. I paid for them because Kelly claimed she left her wallet at home. She had better hand it over as soon as we hit the door. She seemed overly friendly on the way home, as if I was going to forget her debt. I played along by smiling at her stupid conversation about basketball players and their mistresses. She should know not to mess with me, I would out smart her every time.

My hand moved to the doorknob in slow motion, giving Kelly a clue that she had better get prepared to settle her outstanding balance.

"You so funny, sister." She slapped my shoulder and entered first. She scooted down to Mama's room and I followed. Mama was reading *The Food Temptress* with her reading glasses slouched on her nose. She resembled me for a minute, but with a lighter tone. She smelled like pomegranate and she had on a fresh pair of pajamas.

"Wait until you see what we bought you." Kelly could barely get out the lie. My eyebrows rose up, then down. I observed Kelly opening the packages, so I grabbed a brush and stocking cap from Mama's drawer. I smoothed her hair down gently, twisted the long locks, and pinned it on top her head. I shimmy the cap on while Kelly combed the wig back into shape. It seemed natural for me to touch her and she accepted the experience

"Put it on now," I told her.

Kelly eased the human hair on Mama's head. She pressed down the right side and I the left. We moved in front of her to study the outcome.

With much enthusiasm, I said, "Mama, you are gorgeous!" Kelly and I hi five each other. Mama did not say anything, so Kelly handed her a mirror.

She gloated for a second. "I love it!"

"Yes!" We hit hands again, then flopped down on each side of her. We gave her a dual hug and she clutched us both.

"My girls!"

€€€

I woke up the next day somewhat slow. I tossed and turned for three hours before falling asleep. Then I laid on my side in an awkward position, so my body ached. I thought about Mama mostly as well as all the things that I still needed to do before I leave for college in two weeks. I had seen Mama vulnerable the past few days. I was sure that hurt the worst. She had always been strong, smart and mobile. I could not help but think that cancer could be the earth's way of kicking Mama in the face with karma.

"Dana, come quick, something has happened to Mama," Kelly squealed.

I took the stairs by twos until I reached her. She lie face down on the floor and I checked for a pulse, but did not feel one.

"Call 911!"

Kelly did not move, so I shoved her. "Call 911, dammit!"

She snatched Mama's phone from the nightstand. I turned Mama on her back and administered cardiopulmonary resuscitation (CPR). I learned how after I started babysitting on a regular basis. The YMCA offered classes and Mrs. Miller insisted that I take them. I pumped Mama's chest, then I blew into her mouth. I repeated two times before I got indication of life. However, she remained unconscious. I called her name, but she did not respond. Kelly screamed repeatedly at the dispatcher and I could not figure out a word because of her crying. She left the room and a minute later, returned with the paramedics.

"We will take over now. You did well," the skinny man commented.

I moved to the side and watched as they placed Mama on a gurney. Kelly grabbed her lower abdomen and collapsed on the floor with no life in her limbs. A chocolate male tended to her. I was in shock, but I felt confident that Mama would make it. I stayed composed for their sake.

€€€

Mama lay there very still. I could hear the sound of the heart monitor, an annoying piercing sound in one-second intervals. Though Mama's cancer showed signs of remission, it had spread to her lungs and stomach. It was in stage four.

I had just returned from seeing Kelly in the maternity ward upstairs. I finally had her resting peacefully after she learned that her baby died. In route to the hospital, her water broke. Kelly's blood pressure shot up and it put stress on the baby. She named her baby girl, Danail, after me. It meant, "God is my judge."

"I…"

"Save your strength, Mama." I pulled the blanket over her chest.

"I…I..."

"Shh." I tapped her arm with four pats.

Her mouth opened again and I waited for the echo.

"You are a beautiful girl, Dana. I love you."

I could not believe what Mama said to me. I had waited to hear those words my entire life. I did not bother to wipe the tears that cascaded down my face onto the bed. Mama's eyelids seem too heavy for her to pry open, but she managed in three-second maneuvers.

I leaned my head to the right and admired her beauty. I touched her silky black hair, then traced her matching eyebrows with my fingers. I kissed her smooth cheeks and took a deep breath. As soon as I exhaled, so did Mama – her final one.

"I love you, too, Mama."

€€€

I put the final bag in the car. I did not realize how much work went into moving and I only removed stuff from one room. Kelly helped me pack; however, it still took me four hours, minus the half hour reminiscing about Mama and the other half-getting college tips from Kelly. We laughed about Mama always telling us that she had work to do and spending most of her time on the computer in her office. We knew that she was playing around in the chat rooms and on personal sites. We did not say anything because it kept her busy and out of our business.

Then, Kelly warned me about the "Freshmen Fifteen," frat parties, and naughty professors. I looked forward to going to Columbia University and all the experiences it had to offer. My best friends would be nearby if I needed a dose of home and reality.

"Ready?" Kelly scared me when she entered the kitchen.

"Yes." I picked up my purse, then dropped it. I grabbed Kelly and pulled her into my chest. She cried first then I followed suit.

"I better get on the road. I'll call you when I get to my first stop."

"Alright." She wiped her tears with her fingertips. I held her shoulder until we reached the front door. I walked out first and stopped at the bottom of the porch steps. I stared at the red Camry that Mama once owned and that I now drove. I wished that she was here to see me. I had forgiven her for all the pain and heartache that she caused the day that she told us about her cancer.

"I know." Kelly gripped my hand. We approached the car door.

"I love you, Dana."

"I love you, too. I'll see you for Thanksgiving, okay?"

Kelly nodded.

We kissed cheeks and hugged one final time. I smiled and got into the Camry. I watched Kelly wave at me through the rearview mirror.

About the Author

Rekaya Gibson

Rekaya Gibson is an Author, Food Writer, and Researcher living in Virginia. Her other fiction titles include *The Food Temptress, The Food Enchantress* as well as her children's books, *Are There French Fries in Heaven?* and *My Mama's Sweet Potato Pie/El Pay de Camote di mi Mama*. In addition, she writes cookbook reviews for *Cuisine Noir Magazine*, articles for The Food Temptress blog, and restaurant reviews for the All Occasions Eater blog. In her spare time, she photographs nature scenes, delicious foods, and interesting people. For author appearances or more information, contact her at rekaya@rekayagibson.com and become a fan of Author Rekaya Gibson on Facebook.